Route Offline

Short Stories

route 20

First Published by Route in 2008
PO Box 167, Pontefract, WF8 4WW
e-mail: info@route-online.com
web: www.route-online.com

ISBN: 978-1901927368

First Edition

Editors:
Ian Daley, Crista Ermiya, Katherine Locke,
Daithidh MacEochaidh, Susan Tranter

Editorial Support:
Isabel Galan, Emma Smith

Cover Design:
Andy Campbell
www.absolutely-nothing.com

A catalogue for this book is available from the British Library

This book was possible thanks to support from
Arts Council England

Printed and bound in Great Britain by
Biddles Ltd., King's Lynn, Norfolk

Inside

Route Offline brings together five short story collections originally published digitally on www.route-online.com

Dog Days

Dog Days: the ancient Romans noticed that the hottest days of the year, in late July and early August, coincided with the Dog Star being in the same part of the sky as the sun. This powerful collection of stories is scorched with summer heat. An emotional and hazy landscape, *Dog Days* will put a sun tan on your soul. Editor: Katherine Locke

Brief Lives

How can short stories ever give us more than a passing glimpse into other people's lives? What exactly *is* a life story, and how can it be told in so few words? Can short fiction deal with anything more than fragments of time? Here are four stories from four writers which explore some very different lives. In the process, they reveal the capacity of the short story to convey more than snapshots of time. Editor: Susan Tranter

East of No East

East is a term that describes our ignorance. These stories from an Eastern European country, from Bulgaria, from contemporary Bulgarian writers, begin to unwrite the empty token 'exotic' into awareness, understanding and delight. Editor: Daithidh MacEochaidh

Skin

Skin is a border, the porous barrier between what's on the outside and the inside; appearance and reality. The three stories and two non-fiction pieces collected here are outposts on the frontier, each with a different view across the landscape. Editor: Crista Ermiya

The Three and Half Day Parent

A young father is happy to be a split-parent, half a week he looks after his son, the other half of the week he 'does drink'; a situation he advocates as a pragmatic way forward for the future of parenting. In this mini-collection of stories, a series of adult encounters with children in various scenarios have the cumulative effect of strengthening this case. *The Three and a Half Day Parent* is a funny and affectionate look at the relationship between adults and their children and will have you chuckling with recognition from start to finish. Stories by James K Walker

Contents

Dog Days

Editor: Katherine Locke

Introduction
Katherine Locke

Putting together a compilation of short stories around a particular topic is a daunting task. *Dog Days* started as an idea about how we interpret themes in writing and how creative responses can be produced from an everyday phrase. The ancient Romans noticed that the hottest days of the year, in late July and early August, coincided with the Dog Star (aka Sirius, aka The Great Dog) being in the same part of the sky as the sun. They thought the position of the star contributed to the heat of the day. Dog days could also be taken literally, to mean days with dogs. There was plenty of room for interpretation of the title.

What makes a good short story continues to be the subject of much debate. Surely it is very subjective? It is a matter of taste – the individual responding to a particular subject. Up to a point that is the case, one person will love a story that another loathes. However, as far back as the 1830s, Edgar Allan Poe developed a set of six rules for writing a short story that still bear relevance today. They were: a short story should be a complete piece able to stand alone, it must be possible to read it in one sitting, every word must be used to good effect, it should have a strong opening sentence that is developed throughout the work, the story should end at its climax and have no more characters than those necessary for the action.

Although there are many books, classes and courses on what makes a good short story, Poe's six rules still provide pertinent (and concise) advice for any piece of short fiction. The quality of submissions to this compilation made it clear that short story writers are alive and well and fully conversant with Poe's guidelines. The stories included in this compilation have been selected for their success in interpreting the theme, evoking place and demanding an emotional response.

I hope you enjoy them.

The Devil's Music

Jane Rusbridge

Jelly makes a sighing noise, a little whimper, like Honey when she wants to go for a walk.

'They'll be back soon, Jelly. Don't be sad.'

I shiggle her carrycot to make the heebie-jeebies go away.

The sea's right out, thin and flat. No one else on the sand but me and Jelly and Honey on the edge of the pebbles, and a man digging for lugworms a long way away. When Mummy and Susie come back with the ice-creams, I'm going to make an enormous sandcastle with my new spade.

I'm leaving you in charge, Andrew, Mummy said, holding Susie's hand.

Honey chomps and slobbers on a bit of wood. She's wet, the fur on her legs and on her tummy all dark and stuck together like little feathers. She's got her head on one side, chewing, the piece of wood pushed right up into the corner of her mouth, her black lips stretching back to show her gums. Her teeth are long and pointy.

Jelly's whining gets louder. She wriggles on her back as if she's itchy. Her head's right at the top and her feet are right at the bottom of the carrycot. She's much too big and fat for it. Even though she's nearly four, she hasn't stopped being a baby. She cries a lot.

When I was nearly four, Susie was born and I helped Mummy with things like passing Johnson's Baby Powder and lining up the cotton buds. I wonder if Jelly will always be a baby and what it will be like when she's the same size as a grown-up and people call her Elaine, her real name.

I lie on my back to see the same as she sees. Wind blows white bits of cloud across the sky. I practise my whistling. Grampy says that sailors think whistling is the Devil's music. It can call up a storm at sea, or a death by drowning.

Jelly has stopped wriggling. I blow some spit bubbles for her, but she's not watching. 'Now, Jelly,' I lean right over her, my shadow big and dark, 'I've made you a pool and now I'm going to make drip people next to it. Or shall I write your name in the sand?'

We talk to Jelly in questions, same as when we say to Honey, do you want to play ball? And Honey fetches her special tennis ball with no fur left. Or, do you want a choccy-drop? And she stands by the larder door. I put a finger on the place where Jelly's neck joins her chest and stroke the little dip there. Her skin is soft and white. I whisper my question right into her ear, 'Which would you like, Jelly?'

Her head goes from side to side. She's staring at the tassels on the carrycot canopy. I take a deep breath in and blow them, puffing out my cheeks like the wind.

Mummy and Susie are a very long time.

Honey stops chomping. She drops her stick on the pebbles and nudges it, looking sideways at me. Then she sniffs at the stick, wrinkling up her nose to show her teeth. She gives one bark.

I know what she wants, but I'm pretending I don't.

Honey jumps up, brings her stick over and drops it on the pebbles by my feet. Her nose touches my ankle. Wind blows, cold on the wetness. She looks at the stick; me; the stick; her eyebrows twitching.

I pick up a pebble and roll it in my hand. I watch the lugworm man digging his hole.

Honey pushes at my arm with her nose, her pink tongue curling out to give me a lick. She rests her chin on me and looks sad. I put my arms around her and rub her seaweedy fur. On the top of her head where the fur is thin, I can feel her skull.

Suddenly she's up. She leaps around her stick, crouching down and bouncing up, pebbles flying everywhere. The stick's all slimy with slobber when I grab it and run, run onto the hard sand. Honey – chasing, crazy –

overtakes, her body curled like a ball, a bundle of legs, as she gallops towards the sea, skids around and comes back. Another skid and sand sprays up as she turns and gallops off again, her ears blown inside out by the wind.

I fling the stick as hard as I can. Honey races past the man's lugworm bucket. He stops digging and watches the sandfly. He holds a hand above his eyes to look at me, then at Elaine's carrycot on the edge of the pebbles.

I go back.

Jelly's eyes are closed now and her hand is next to her nose as if she's trying to breathe in her own smell. *She's not all there, Andrew.* I put my face right down to hers, but all I can smell is the hot plastic of the sides of the carrycot.

I don't like strangers looking at Jelly.

I'm going to write her real name in the sand with my new spade.

On Saturday night, Auntie Jean and Mummy talked about Elaine when I was in bed and they thought I couldn't hear. Mummy was crying again. They said about her going away into a Home, and I thought of Gladys at school who has warts on her fingers and smells like leftover gravy. She lives at the Barnardo's Home. We whisper 'Fleabags' behind our hands. I'd rather be dead than be like Gladys.

My new spade is red metal with a wooden handle. It's got a sharp edge that cuts through the sand. Susie has my old spade. It's small and rubbery with swirls of red and blue and green like plasticine colours rolled together.

I carve an E in the sand, five paces high and three paces wide. By the time I've drawn the bottom line of the E, the top line has gone blurry, rubbing itself out. I stand and paddle my feet up and down, up and down on the sand to make sinking sand. Real sinking sand comes when you're not expecting it and suddenly you're up to your ankles in slime. Sometimes there are hard bits under your feet, the bones of people who've drowned. I paddle more. My feet sink lower and lower until cold sand rings my ankles and my feet are deep under heavy wetness. Now Elaine's 'E' has melted back into the sand.

The man digging for lugworms has thrown Honey's stick for her but she brings it back to me. He starts digging a new round hole. My hole has nearly filled up with sand and water again so I kneel over and use my arms to heave out more sand. It slides over my bare legs. When I take my soggy jumper off, the chilly wind gives me goosebumps.

I make my hole deeper, but water and sand come back to fill it. I have to be much faster. The metal disc with Honey's name on it jingles on her collar as she jumps and leaps all around me. She starts to dig with me, her paws flying. Sand sprays up between her back legs. I copy her, cupping my hands, chucking sand between my legs; panting.

If Elaine is not all here, like Mummy says to people, there must be a part of her that is somewhere else. Grampy says Granny is in a better place. Really, she's dead. I know, because we visit her headstone in the graveyard and leave flowers there. But Grampy still talks to her and blows a goodbye kiss.

Elaine starts again with her whimpers. I feel sorry that she just lies in the carrycot and can't get out and play with us in the sand so I shiggle the sides of the carrycot a bit more to try and make her laugh. She doesn't do her giggle much any more, even when I lick the bottoms of her feet. Mummy says she's sore somewhere, they don't know where. I think they mean in her head. She wears nappies still, so perhaps it's them that make her sore. Or perhaps she's hungry because she only has milk from a bottle or sometimes mushed up food. No nice food like chocolate, or even Parma violets which are only little. I thought she'd like them.

Now she's crying and coughing with a sound like she's going to be sick. I still can't see Mummy and Susie coming back from the ice-cream van. I push the canopy back and see that Elaine's head is squashed right up at the top of the carrycot and her hair is stuck down and wet with sweat. I put my hands under her arms and try to sit her up. She's heavy and very wobbly. She can't sit up by herself yet.

She takes a deep breath in. Her face goes red. She opens her mouth wide and screams. I lay her down again.

I'll have to wash the sand off. She's different from me and doesn't like the feel of sand on her skin, which I do know already so I wish I hadn't touched her with my sandy hands. I lick one of her fat feet and explain how to make sand go soft by pressing down so that the water comes through, or by squeezing the sand in your fist. That's how to make drip people, I tell her, but her mouth is big and wet and red with screaming.

Honey has gone for a swim. Her head is a dot in the water.

Elaine doesn't stop screaming even when I play Boo! over the side of the carrycot.

The man digging holes is looking again.

I'll fetch some nice clear water in the bucket to wash the sand off her and stop her being so hot and cross. I tip Susie's slipper shells out of the bucket. I'll have to run because I'm not supposed to leave Elaine. I'm in charge. The tide is far out, the sea a grey line.

Honey comes back from the sea and starts shaking her head from side to side. I grab her collar and drag her away from Elaine just as she starts to twist her whole body faster and faster and seawater droplets fly out, spreading everywhere and spattering me.

Now Honey's here, I can go. I spread my towel on the sand. Elaine is heavy, but I just manage to lift her out of the carrycot. I lay her on her back. She stops crying and gasps a little bit, screwing up her eyes because the sky is big and bright even though the sun keeps going behind the clouds. She stops crying and kicks her legs like she's happy.

The bucket is full to the brim but water sloshes out when I run, so I have to go back to fill it up again. This time I walk, watching the water in the bucket, my legs moving straight and hard. Ripples of sand press into my feet. Splashes of water spill and leave dark patches on my salty-white skin.

I'm on the flat sand now and I can see Honey trotting in a circle, round and round Elaine and Mummy walking across the pebbles with the ice-creams, taking huge steps because she doesn't want them to melt. Susie is left behind. She stops and shakes her head, holds up her arms. What a cry baby.

Elaine is probably even more sandy now because I can see that she has rolled over onto her tummy to play on the heap of wet sand by my pool. I am pleased that she has done that. Honey stops going round and round and sits down next to her. She points her nose in the air and starts to bark, loud.

The lugworm man throws down his spade and he's running past me, his hands pumping like he's trying to win a race.

Mummy reaches my pool and, for a second, she stands very straight. My tummy slops downwards. The ice-creams fall out of her hands onto the sand. Honey dips her nose to them. Mummy scoops Elaine up and wraps her arms round her. Mummy lifts her face up to the sky and her mouth is in a big O with a high sound that doesn't stop.

When We Talk About Words

Carla Gericke

My friend Cassandra Vermeulen was talking. 'Remember when people still cared about which word to use?' she asked as she built A-C-O-R-N-S across on a Double Word Score. 'Nuances,' she said, adding her 'S' to my 'SKIN'. 'Or, wait, let's table nuances for a moment. Let's start with something easy. Like martyr versus terrorist. Or, necklacing.'

The doors to the pool were open and I could smell wet cut grass, from the gardener earlier and the late afternoon drizzle. The four of us sat around her dining room table, me and Cassie and Bob, my best friend and her husband, and Lakshmi, my second wife, a software developer I met in Vegas. Since Lakshmi was originally from India and Cassie from South Africa, Bob and me liked to joke about being two Texans who had bedded and wedded their way right into the U.N.

Red and white wine bottles stood on the table. White for Cassie and me, red for Bob and Lakshmi. I could never hold my red. Puts me in a fighting mood, and, after I plucked all the keys off my laptop with a screwdriver late one night before stabbing it into the wall, I vowed never to drink red again.

'That's,' Cassie counted on her fingers, 'twenty-five.'

Bob was keeping tally. Before he could write her score, Lakshmi said, 'Skins? Plural? I don't think so. One skin per person.'

'We skinned a bobcat once,' Bob said. 'Remember that, Jack? Back in high school? Out near Willow's Creek? Ya'll read about the fellah in Montana who caught the plague skinning one? Not too long ago.'

'Skins,' I said and nodded to show I did remember, it was something I would never forget, 'present tense "to skin", as in "Hannibal Lector skins his next victim".'

'The plague?' Lakshmi wrinkled her nose. 'That old thing it is still going around? And, never mind,' her bangles tinkled when she waved her hand, 'I retract my objection, skins of many colours. Like us.' She smiled, her sharp, little teeth flashed against her dark skin. She flipped her ponytail over her shoulder. Her sandals were kicked off under her chair. She had a tiny silver toe-ring on.

'Also, "skins",' Cassie narrowed her eyes at Bob, 'to fleece or swindle. Case in point,' she tapped his arm, gesturing that he should record her score. 'Twenty-five, mate.'

Cassie used to be a lawyer – she'd been doing something at the Truth and Reconciliation Commission when she met Bob, who'd gone out there to write about it for *The Times* – and, even though she edited books now, she still likes to hold court.

'Twenty-five,' she repeated and tapped Bob's arm again. 'No cheating.'

Cassie was a tall, beautiful woman who was starting to go soft. Nothing serious, just a little out of focus, a little more flesh on her chin and upper arms than there used to be. A line of fine dark hairs ran from her bush to her navel. I knew because we went skinny-dipping together last fall. The three of us had been out by the pool, drinking, barbecuing – Lakshmi was working late – when Cassie asked me who the oldest mother in the world was. I said it had to be a broad in China or India. She insisted it was some woman in Italy who'd had *in vitro*. 'But, the real question is,' she said before pushing me into the pool, 'who's the oldest mother fucker?' When I came up for air, she was unhooking her bra. 'The turkey-baster did it, Yerronner,' I yelled and stripped off my wet clothes. They landed with a thunk on the tiles near Bob, who was standing by the grill. Cassie jumped in, aiming for my head. I ducked. When I surfaced, I glanced around for Bob. He was watching us from the edge of the pool, snapping his tongs. When I looked over again later, he had turned back to the meat.

'Fleece?' Bob said now, and, as he recorded Cassie's score, he started to sing in a childlike voice. 'Baa-baa Black Plague, have you any more?'

'Any more?' Cassie asked. 'Isn't it "any wool"?' Regardless, let's take that as an example. Do children even learn nursery rhymes any more? When our friends – the ones with kids – visit, they always arrive with armfuls of DVDs, not books. Are parents still reading to their kids? Or is it just big fat purple monsters and gay thingamajiggies with purses?'

'But,' Bob said, 'Video did *not* kill the radio star. Look at satellite radio. Huge. It ain't right to say technological advances are killing literature.'

'And look at our half-baked hooligan,' Lakshmi said. 'We know he, at least, reads nursery rhymes. My Pet Goat –'

'– Read by Incurious George,' Cassie said.

'Hey, now,' Bob protested, but we all laughed anyway. I stood up and poured more wine. When I reached Lakshmi, she put her hand over her glass and said, 'Speaking of ki –'

'– If I had another "D" and a "U"' – Bob looked up from his tiles at Cassie – 'I could spell "Luddite".'

'One,' Cassie ticked off on her fingers as she spoke, 'Luddite is a proper noun. Two, spell "tide" or "lithe" – do you have an "H"?' She leaned over the table to peek at his tiles but he held his hand over her eyes and she sat back down. 'And, three, I'm not a Luddite. I'm just saying that people are in danger of becoming even bigger bloody bozos than they already are. I mean, if we did a Google search, imagine the idiotic things we'd find under "The Dumbest Thing I Ever Did".'

'There's the rub, though,' Bob said and moved his tiles around on his tray. '"If we did a Google search". Means you're using technology – a technology you have to be able to read and write to use, I might add – to learn more. And that ain't bad.' I nodded in agreement. Cassie twisted her earring and tilted her head. Lakshmi wriggled in her chair and sighed. 'In fact,' he continued, 'it's good. Ya'll see that *Times* article a while back? About how people are getting smarter?'

I shook my head. 'What'd it sa –'

'– You guys seen *Dog Day Afternoon*?' Cassie interrupted, turning towards Lakshmi. 'Old Pacino movie where he plays a gay guy who robs a bank to get money to pay for his lover's sex change? Well, it was based on a true story. We went to see this documentary about it at the film festival last week – and the first thing the director says, is, when it happened – this was way back in the Seventies – no one wanted to touch it. No one wanted to make *Dog Days* because they thought it was too weird, too unbelievable, too "facts stranger than fiction". But, don't you think, when something's true, when it's not some made-up crap, you get a bigger thrill? Isn't it more tantalising to know it's real? And, *here's the rub*, this guy, the gay robber –'

'– Robbing Hood –'

'– Rubbing Wood –'

'– Hoodwinked Wo –'

'– Guys! In the documentary, this guy, this, this, okay, okay, I'll play, this Wood-Rubbing Tinky-Winky, takes stuff from the movie, stuff the Hollywood screenwriters made up for dramatic effect – said so themselves – and says these things happened to him. He appropriates things *from the movie* to make himself seem more compelling. Things that never even happened. Isn't that crazy?'

'But,' Bob glanced up from the board, 'now you're contradicting yourself. You can't say on the one hand, truth is the only way, and then say the made-up parts, the fiction, is better.'

Cassie swirled her wine. 'Well, yes, I suppose.' She held her glass high over her head and said, "Tis one of the disadvantages of wine, makes *this* woman mistake words for thought.'

'Nice,' I said. Her words reminded me of the first woman – girl, really – I'd slept with. Belinda Perry – a world removed from Lakshmi Joshipura – would whisper poetry in my ear while we fucked, standing up, on her parents' basement stairs. We'd considered ourselves so grown-up, but they were childish lines to match our childish fumbling, 'double, double,' kind of stuff. I smiled at the memory.

'Johnson, methinks,' Cassie said, returning my smile. 'Did you know there are now less people who *read* poetry than who actually *write* it?

That's what I'm talking about. Where are the readers? It's all about supply and demand. And the demand – the reader – is missing. Ergo –'

'– But even if demand for fiction is missing,' Bob said, 'it ain't missing for the things that actually interest folks. That article I was trying to tell you about said folks' brains are evolving in ways that allow them to process more and more complex information. More complex plots, sub-plots, characters. Look at video games. Interactive storytelling, right there. There's a plot and you get to write your own ending based on your skills. No wonder kids ain't reading any more. It's boring.'

'Once, when we went back home to South Africa, we visited friends of ours – mine – out near Cape Town. Guess what happened? Bob here, spent, what was it? Two whole days, *two whole days*, and nights, mind you, he didn't sleep a wink, playing their kids' video games. Sat in the study all by his lonesome. Ignored us flat-out.' Cassie crossed her arms and scowled at Bob.

'Ah, yes, civilisation, I remember it well.'

'Bloody uncivilised Yankee.'

'Whoa there, ma'am. I ain't no Yankee. Nosiree, not this Bob.' He pretended to doff a hat at her. 'And, ya know, that kinda talk could get a bolshy lady like yerself killed out here in these parts.'

'Ballsy?'

'Bolshy.'

'No such word.'

'Try.' He shoved the dictionary across the table at her. 'But I can save you the trouble. Means obstreperous. Or do you need to look *that* up?'

'Dog days of summer,' Lakshmi said with a sidelong glance at me. 'What a beautiful phrase. I wonder where it came from? Because dogs died when it got too hot? Or because you felt like a dog? Like a bitch in heat?' She laughed. 'I'm trying to recall whether it is something we say in India. I should email my brother and ask. You guys have wireless? Can I borrow your laptop?'

'Ethical,' Bob said and laid his tiles on the board. He nodded at Lakshmi. 'Thirty-six.'

'Nice one,' I said and glanced at the board. Bob had laid his tiles where I was planning to play. I'd have to find a new space. I liked to plan ahead, to figure my spot before my turn. Meant I got shot down a lot. Sometimes, I wondered why I bothered. For those rare instances I didn't get fouled up? For the challenge? To try and try again? Or just plain old-fashioned personal perversion? Probably.

'What's yours?' Lakshmi looked at me. 'The Dumbest Thing You Ever Did?'

'So,' Cassie said to Bob, 'you *did* have an aitch, Dear Henry.'

'Indeed, Dear Liza. And, come to think of it, one, from the bottom of my heart,' Bob overemphasised the 'h', 'thanks for the "A", came in handy, and, two,' he calculated the last round, 'I'm now officially whupping your ass.'

'Baba, look,' Lakshmi said with a grin, 'a spanking at two-o-clock.'

'That's "whipping",' Cassie said.

'Not in Texas, it ain't.' Bob stood up abruptly. 'More booze? I need to take a leak.'

As he strode from the room, Cassie raised her glass at his back and said, 'To my whipping boy.' I watched a drop of wine roll down her chin and plunk onto her breast. My gaze lingered for a moment before sliding away. Outside, it looked like more rain.

'What was it?' Lakshmi asked when Bob placed the laptop on the table in front of her. He made to fill her glass, but she shook her head and he moved on.

'The dumbest thing?' Bob's one hand rested on Cassie's shoulder as he poured her more wine. 'Besides falling in love with this one?' Cassie tipped her head back to look up at him. He hesitated for a moment then kissed the tip of her nose. 'I'd have to say the bobcat incident is right up th –'

'– Whose turn is it?' I said, frowning. 'Lakshmi, play.'

Lakshmi grimaced and arched her back. When she settled down, her hands rested on her stomach. I snatched the faded pillowcase and jangled the letters inside. When Bob sat down, I thrust the bag at him. He looked at me, surprised. I shook my head. I didn't want to talk about that day. Didn't want to think about it. I was disgusted by what we – I – had done. I'd wanted to be able to hunt, to kill, to be like my Pa, my Grandpa, my friends, like Bob. I'm a Texan, for chrissake. But I'd hated it. And I hadn't wanted Bob to know.

Lakshmi bit her bottom lip as she stared at her tiles. 'Why,' she asked, 'Do I always get the "Q" but never the "U"?'

That late summer day when we shot the bobcat, it squirmed and mewled at our feet. When we gutted its swollen belly, six kittens had slithered out with its guts and blood and shit into the dust. They were almost full-term and alive, writhing blindly on the ground. I hadn't known what to do.

'I love the "Q",' Cassie said. 'And there are words you can build without a "U".'

Standing in the hot sun, I'd looked over at Bob and, when, with one eyebrow cocked, he ran his finger across his throat and laughed, a wave of shame came over me, for not knowing what to do, for not wanting to kill them, for having shot their mama. My shame turned to anger. Anger at the shame.

'Like what?' Lakshmi asked.

Afterwards, I wished there was a way to reverse what I had done. A death like that was too – what was the word? – cruel? – no, too – wanton. I moved my 'W' next to my 'A.' I didn't have any of the other letters.

'Iraq,' Bob said.

The women groaned.

'You know the rule,' Cassie said and pointed towards the empty wine bottles. 'No politics after three.'

Droplets clung to the outside of the white wine bottle. The curtain whipped up and blew into the room, like a blind man's fingers groping for something to hold.

'More rain's on the way,' I said.

It was turning dark outside and I could barely make out the silhouette of the cactus, past the pool near the fence. The room was already too dark, but it was that time of day, that type of day where none of us wanted the light on. A light would make us real. It would bring us back into the world. Right now, there were only the four of us, with our wine and words. We had a game to play.

I turned to Cassie and to distract myself, I decided to get her going. 'Do you really think literature is dying?'

'I'm not sure.' She put her glass down and stretched her arms out on the table, palms up. 'But let me ask you this, how many books have you read this year? No, not books, actual novels. For the past few years, I've been reading more non-fiction – 'Who Moved the Cheese' crap, or memoirs – than Nabokov. In fact, at work, because non-fiction sells better these days, I'm only editing memoirs. We're still publishing our current stable, but we're not taking on any new lit writers. And, I have to confess, I like the idea of knowing *this* story about *this* cripple midget in a golden Velcro suit who makes his living by going to bars and getting tossed against a giant portable Velcro dartboard, is true.'

'That is a real book?' Lakshmi's eyebrows almost reached her bangs.

Cassie shook her head. 'No, but soon, I bet.' She twisted her earring again. 'With literacy improving and modern technology – see? I'm not a Luddite – everyone can now tell their story. Think about it, why, way back when, did people read novels? Because they were seeking something familiar. What's it called, again? Those "little moments of truth." Those "a-ha moments," in today's terms, where you recognize something about yourself, where you go, "Okay, I'm not a total freak" –'

'– Says you,' Bob said.

'– "There are other people just like me. I'm not alone." But, it's all been done. There are no more surprises. Unrequited love?' – Cassie started to tick off on her fingers – 'Shakespeare. Medieval melodrama? Chaucer. There's Dickens. And Hemingway. And J.D. and Marquez and

Joyce – Joyce really stuffed things up. Looking for a story about people like us? Sitting around a table, talking crap and getting hammered? There's whatshisface' – she sliced her hand through the air – 'Carver. And, Luddite or not, television has had a massive influence. Especially reality TV. Just like the memoir. Why's the truth so popular? Because, now, people can either, one, see themselves, or, two, be entertained by the "freaks" –'

I looked at Bob and could see he was thinking the same thing I was. He nodded and together we broke into an off-key version of the chorus of *Superfreak*. Lakshmi laughed. Cassie ignored us and continued to talk over our singing.

'– Because that's it, either you want to recognise something in yourself, or you want to reassure yourself that you're better than everyone else. It's all about ego, it's "all about me" – and, look – even if those shows are edited for maximum entertainment value, the studios are getting better value for money. Look at how much they have to pay the big schlebs these days. No wonder the studios are moving towards real people, real people desperate for their Campbell moment – only, today, like soup, it's fifteen seconds, not minutes. It's a simple cost-benefit analysis. It doesn't take a genius to see –'

'– But,' Bob interrupted.

'No, wait, let me finish.'

'Com'on, Cass,' Bob said. 'You ain't arguing in front of a judge, you know.'

'Oh, aren't I?' Cassie said sarcastically. She picked up her glass and sat back with a sweep of her arm. 'All yours, then.'

'Never mind. Talk, or I'll be watching that lip all night.'

Cassie grimaced at Bob, took a deep breath, sat forward and said, 'Okay, I'll be quick. In the past, because of geographic limitations, and the lack of technology, people had to make up stories about "Lands far, far away". Magical lands. Enchanted forests. Faraway trees. God, I loved those stories. I'd imagine myself floating away on my mattress after a flood, travelling on all these adventures. My dog and I, Machiavelli – that was really his name, my folks were ridiculously pretentious – would float through town after town on my mattress, like Huck Finn. But now? Now, we hop on a bloody plane, or rocketship, and *go* to that land, or to the moon. Or pop in a DVD and *see* that land. Now, we simply log onto the Internet and *voila!* Knowledge at your fingertips.' She wiggled her fingers in the air. It looked as though there were tears in her eyes.

'Jesus, Cass,' Bob reached across the table and clasped her wrist. 'Are you drunk?'

'Tell me if I'm wrong.' A tear rolled down her cheek. 'Tell me.' She pulled her arm free and threw her hands in the air. 'What do I know?' She rubbed her cheek with the heel of her hand. 'That's just how it seems to me.' She took a sip of wine and placed her glass back on the table. 'I proclaim,' she said, finger in the air, 'that fiction is dead. Time of death, ladies and gentlemen,' she looked at her wristwatch, '5:48pm.'

'But, but,' Lakshmi said and I could tell she was working her toe-ring under the table, 'that's like proclaiming the end of imagination. It's like saying Tinkerbell never existed – I know she didn't, but, you know what I mean – what you're saying, is, it is like you're Peter Pan. The Peter Pan who has to believe in order to fly. You have to learn to fly again. You have to *believe*.'

'You know what?' Cassie turned towards Lakshmi. 'I didn't like you much when Jack first brought you here –'

'– Cass!' Bob said.

'– I thought you were just some floozy. A phase.'

'Well, I didn't much care for you either, to be honest.'

'Really?' Cassie tilted her head. 'Yes, I suppose I can see that. I am, as Bob and Jack will tell you, an acquired taste. But' – she held up her hand to stop me from interrupting – 'I never liked Nancy, sorry Jack, but that's the truth. She's one cold cunt. The Fucking Ice Queen of Texas. The Big Chill. Brrrrrrrr.' She pretended to shiver. 'Remember how she refused to have kids? Used it as blackmail. Jack wanted to have children – *I* wanted to have children – did you know that? How many, three? Four?'

'You wanted to have Jack's children?' Lakshmi said with a tight smile. She looked over at Bob with one eyebrow raised, then at me and said, 'I knew it.' The edge to her voice made it impossible to tell whether she was joking or not. Bob looked down at his hands.

'Speaking of queens,' I said and reached over to rub Lakshmi's arm, 'how about you take your turn?' Soon after the company off-site in Vegas, we had run into each other in the hallway at work and Lakshmi said: 'What happens in Vegas sometimes leaves Vegas and sits in a cubicle not far from your office, not so, Mister Boss Man?' She'd waggled her head at me in that peculiar way people from India do, and, at that moment, I knew I would marry her. The Ice Queen was not amused. 'Thank God we never had kids,' she said. 'And, I'm taking the Corvette.'

'You could have, you know,' Bob said now. I glanced at him. He was watching Cassie. 'Had kids.'

'How? With another man? With Jack? When? Between wives? Was there even an in-between? *You're* my bloody husband. For better or worse, sperm-less wonder that you are, and all.'

'For chrissake,' I said. 'Don't start you two.'

'Let her talk, Baba. I don't mind. That is how we women are sometimes. We have to say what it is on our minds. Try to stop her now and it'll be "whhrrrrreerrr".' Lakshmi made little claws with her hands. I wondered whether she was consciously copying Cassie. Lakshmi was smart that way. 'And,' she added, 'for future reference, I'm not a queen, I'm an honest-to-God, "god".' She made a temple with her palms and swayed her body like a snake charmer. It worked.

Cassie smiled at Lakshmi and turned to me. 'You found a good one this time, Jackie-Boy. Young, but good. Which is what I was trying to say in my roundabout way.'

'That's your problem, Cass,' Bob said. 'You always focus on the negative first. We've talked about this. Here, in our country, we say, 'I like you but –'

'– "Here in our country?"' Cassie and Lakshmi said in unison and laughed. Cassie scraped back her chair and sauntered over to Lakshmi. She stood behind her chair, threw her arms around her neck and whispered something in her ear. Lakshmi giggled, put her hand in front of her mouth and nodded. Bob looked over at me, his head cocked as though to say: girl-on-girl action. Or maybe that was just what I was thinking. Cassie kissed Lakshmi on the cheek and, with a sad smile I didn't understand, reached over her shoulder to rearrange her tiles. Cassie stood back and said, 'I'm peckish.' She rested her hands on Lakshmi's shoulders and squeezed them gently. 'You guys hungry?'

'Water for me,' Lakshmi said.

'Snack stuff's in the fridge,' Bob said. 'And bring more booze.'

'Is it my turn yet?' Cassie asked when she returned carrying a tray laden with cheese and crackers and fruit. Two wine bottles balanced each end and a solitary glass of water stood between the plates. 'God, it's dark in here. Shall I turn on the light?'

'No,' I said.

'No,' she sighed. 'I suppose not.'

We dove into the food. I was suddenly starving. Knives clanked against our plates as we ate. Lakshmi drank her water and started to type. The keys clicked beneath her nails. In the distance, I could hear thunder rumble.

'I was just thinking in the kitchen,' Cassie said. She held a small bunch of grapes in her palm. 'Do you guys have a favourite word?' She lobbed a grape into her mouth, it missed, and at that moment, she looked like a clumsy tomboy. 'I get "Word of the Day" emails and sometimes there's a word that just grabs me, reaches inside and takes a-hold of me. Or is that a silly question? Like when someone asks you what your favourite book is? I hate that question! How can anyone ask that? It depends. Depends on my mood and my memory.' She laughed. 'God, I *am* drunk. Listen to me.' She bent over to pick up the grape.

'Here it is,' Lakshmi said, looking up from the laptop. 'Dog days.' She started to read from the screen. 'Hot, sultry weather. Ancient times, here we go. Connecting the dots. Stars. Constellations. Bears, Gemini, Canis Major and Canis Minor. Dogs. The big dog, Sirius –'

'– Here, Sirius, Sirius,' Bob called out and whistled.

'Oh, be serious,' Cassie snapped before she realised her inadvertent joke. As we laughed, Bob caught her eye and whistled again. A long, wild, wolf whistle. He wiggled his eyebrows at her. The corners of her eyes crinkled in response. They reached across the table and intertwined their fingers. Bob ran his thumb over her wrist.

'– Was very bright. The ancient people thought the star radiated heat and that, since it shone most brightly during the summer months, it, together with the sun, caused the extra hot weather. Hence "dog days".'

There was a flash of lightning outside. Raindrops started to patter on the roof. As the thunder clapped, Cassie let go of Bob's hand, pushed back her chair and said, 'I need some air.' She got up, walked to the door and leaned against the jamb. One by one, Bob first, we rose to join her.

The four of us stood together in the doorway and watched the raindrops plop into the pool. The big, fat ones that sometimes fall first. Like brave pioneers, or suicidal elders.

'That's one,' Cassie said after a while.

'One what?' I asked.

'One of my favourite words.'

'Raindrops?'

'Cat's-paws.'

Bob put his arm around Cassie. I put my arm around Lakshmi. Bob and me stood shoulder to shoulder.

'That's what you call it when air ruffles the surface of calm water. Cat's-paws.' Cassie skipped her fingers out into the air. 'Like an imaginary cat chasing invisible dragonflies across the water.'

We stood, silently, huddled together under the eaves, listening to the drumming rain. The surface of the pool started to churn.

Lakshmi held her hand out into the rain and said, 'Cats and dogs.' Raindrops splattered onto us. She pulled her hand in and dried it on her jeans. 'That reminds me,' she readjusted herself under the crook of my arm and tipped her head to look up at me, 'what's the story with the bobcat? The Dumbest Thing You Ever Did?'

'The story is,' I said and tightened my hand on her shoulder. I paused for a long time, thinking about that summer day years ago when I'd used the butt of my rifle to crush those poor kittens one by yowling one. I stared out into the rain. When the raindrops slowed down and only the little 'uns still fell, I spoke.

'The story is,' I said again, 'to watch something die is a terrible thing.'

Missy

Joby Williams

The Orion bucks against the breaking sea, and Marvin struggles to hold her steady. His feet drag along the sand as the waves buffet him toward the shore. He is waist deep in water.

He lifts the polystyrene cooler, ice-heavy – maybe a metre long – to his chest and Sion takes it from him at the stern and stows it in the back hatch. Marvin passes a ruddy red petrol container onto his shoulder and turns to the beach.

'Come Missy.'

Missy is working her way around the grounded boats, nose to the floor.

'Come now.'

She turns at his voice, wags a thin brown tail and slopes down to the shoreline, launching herself into the water. Marvin lifts her before she is caught by a wave and carries her like a dish. He offers her up to Sion who puts a hand under each front shoulder and hoists her like a child into the boat.

Missy slides uneasily along the deck, her claws have no purchase on the shiny wooden surface and her legs tremble as the boat dips drunkenly to the sand. She clambers between the rungs of the short metal ladder which lies horizontally across the bow, so that the waves cannot push her too far to the left or right.

As Marvin gives the boat a final running push and lifts himself aboard, Sion steers hard out into the harbour. The village's low huts and dark figures soon lose their definition as they speed away from land. The lanky palms are last to surrender their shape.

Missy and Marvin travel this way together every single day of the year save Sundays, Christmas Day and the three days of Carnival when Marvin flies to Trinidad to stay with his uncle and parties so hard that he forgets that he's a fisherman, forgets that his house has been half-built for six years and so he still has to live with his mother. He almost forgets about Missy.

Missy's mother, Jude, was a saggy-teated bitch who lived on café scraps above Heavenly Bay. Debbie – from the Heavenly Bay Beach Bar – joked one day during Jude's seventh litter that Marvin needed someone to take home and hold on to for once. And, heart full of Old Oak Rum, Marvin accepted and that night he swam home with Missy across the bay.

But Missy was not at home on the water, and so this sweet drunken adoption had condemned her to a life of salt in her eyes, a trembling in her legs and a sickness in her stomach. Only Marvin wouldn't see it, she was his companion and his sea dog.

As *The Orion* rounds the bluff at Pigeon Point, Sion casts out two lines from the back of the boat. The bamboo rods are secured into rope clasps, and they curve to form symmetrical arcs as the wire cuts into the sea.

On a good day in January, when the seas are at their roughest, and winds are up, Marvin and Sion hope to catch eight or nine big fish. Kingfish and tuna swim the waters on this southwestern tip, and sell for $10TT a pound.

As a boy Marvin worked at the fish hut, slicing, gutting and washing each evening at the counter that fronts Main Bay. When the bloodied water had been drained from the cooler, the fish were laid out in order of size along the bench. He would take each one, left hand beneath the gills and right hand circling the trunk of the tail and run his eyes up and down the stiff, shiny body, feeling the scales hard as armour against the palms of his hands.

A knife was sharpened and handed to him and in one movement he would remove each tough fin, exposing the first glimpse of dark flesh. Next he hacked off the mouth and snout, to give it a stable base on which to balance as he held her tail and sliced the belly open. He would lay her down and pull apart her ribs with both hands, dark blood spilling onto his wrists and arms as he tore out her innards. The blood was cold from the icy water of the cooler but the organs were usually still warm and soft. He would hand the tripe to Dexter who bagged it for his mother's soup and the rest would be thrown into a bucket beneath the counter. Next he would place her on her side and slice her into even steaks – hard bones of the ribcage cracking – which he placed onto the scales. These steaks were taken up and sold to the crowd which surrounded him, waving notes and plastic fish bags, and batting flies away from faces. Then he would move on to the next one.

Marvin hasn't cut and sliced in the fish hut for nine years but he remembers how he liked it. He was fast and precise and he knew that the crowd liked to watch him work.

The lines lunge back simultaneously and Sion cuts the engine, bringing a sudden lurch and a shower of spray from the rolling surf. Missy's dull squinting eyes rise from behind a ladder rung and she turns a shaking head to look out into the water. Some yellow foam has appeared at the right side of her mouth and as a wave tips the boat down and sideways she chokes some liquid vomit onto the deck. Marvin is looking the other way, toward two thrashing barracudas that are being reeled jerkily in from the sea.

The fish are unhooked and placed in the cooler, and Sion reworks the bamboo rods.

Marvin and Sion bought *The Orion* together. She had belonged to Sion's brother, but he had moved to Speyside and invested in a glass-bottomed boat for taking tourists around the reef. She had been left neglected and out of water for two months, and the first day that she was theirs, they stripped her and sanded her in the full heat of the day. They painted her red and deep yellow and at sunset they sat side by side on plastic chairs with thin paintbrushes in their hands and wrote her name in long, slender letters on her hull. Marvin had had to keep shooing Missy from the boat so that she didn't brush up against the paintwork, but she sat with them when they had finished and they watched the pelicans dive for fish as the sky got dark.

By midday three kingfish are lying alongside the barracuda in the cooler and Marvin reaches into his bag for some cheese snacks and rips open the pack. He makes his way forward to sit beside Missy who puts her chin on his knee, eyes closed, and he feeds her the chips, wiping the orange dust onto his shorts. Missy just takes one, the rest she flips out of her mouth with her tongue and they lie on Marvin's lap and fall into a salty puddle on the floor of the boat.

Marvin met a girl in August. He had been looking for about a year. He was of the opinion that, at thirty, with some money saved and a house under construction, it was time to shack up. Jaenell had been born in Castara, but moved to Trinidad with her grandmother when she was six years old. Marvin was older, and did not remember her. She came back to the village because she had just had a baby and she wanted to show him where she had grown up.

Now, Jaenell having a child was not an ideal situation, but her husband had left her and now she was single, and pretty and the baby was cute and quiet too. They had got talking one evening, sitting on barrels and drinking beer with her cousins and Sion, and he had asked her to come for a boat ride the next day. Marvin was shy, but the beers in his belly and the sweetness of Jaenell made him brave and he asked her, and after she said yes he rested his hand on his hair and was shy again.

They took the boat to Englishman's Bay the next day. Marvin steered while Jaenell, the baby and Missy rode upfront. He helped her ashore and on the beach he collected sticks and made a fire and barbecued barracuda steaks and they talked about Trinidad.

She was due to fly back the next day and he borrowed Sion's jeep and drove her to the airport. He carried her bags for her and waited while she checked in and then he walked her up to the gate. She leaned up, baby between them, and kissed his cheek, and she put the palm of her hand against his chest and looked at him and said goodbye and that she hoped he would call her. He said that he would, only his voice was croaky, so he cleared his throat and then she had gone.

Marvin didn't see Jaenell again. He called the next night and her grandmother answered the phone and was cold and said that she was sleeping. When he tried to call the following weekend her grandmother said that she had gone to visit her brother in the city. Marvin was embarrassed to keep speaking to this lady and so he called just one more time, late one evening after too much rum, and her grandmother must have heard the urgency in his voice and she told him not to call again.

The sun sears Marvin's coffee skin and salt from the sea and from his sweat make white tornados on his arms.

He has two scars on his left shoulder that shine liquid stitching. He and Missy had walked together up to the waterfall behind the football field one hot Sunday last year, hopping from rock to mossy rock along the river bed into the jungle. The deep fresh pool caught the sun and beckoned them in and Marvin spied a thick vine spiralling down from a fallen trunk suspended above them. He tugged it sharply, testing its strength, and then once more, letting it take his weight for a few seconds. The vine held and the trunk did not budge.

Marvin stood on a flat rock, a half-metre tall and gripped the vine high up and tightly between his hands, and, with a Tarzan howl, he launched himself into the water. He heard the dull crack midway through the air and felt the log shift and himself falling. Scrabbling to position his body above the water to save his bones, he left his shoulder behind, and it was this that the falling trunk landed upon, pinning him to the floor. Missy had sat beside him and yelled so loud that three kids playing football had heard and followed the sound to a bleeding, fractured Marvin and a worried dog who rode with him in the truck all the way to the hospital in Crowne Point.

Marvin points the boat out towards the shallow pool, two kilometres from the shore and glimmering turquoise. He drops anchor. Sion likes to stop here to collect sand for his aquarium. He duck-dives and emerges with fists dripping dark, runny sea bed which he thrusts into an empty ice-cream tub tied to the anchor rope.

Marvin bounces in too, tumbling gracelessly beneath the water in the way that makes him feel the most free. He surfaces and calls for Missy. She likes to swim. He calls again, twice more, but her sandy head does not appear above *The Orion*'s rim. 'Come now Miss, fresh up.' He wades up to the boat and peers over the stern. He can see her curled frame bobbing up and down on the front deck, his heart quickens and his stomach bobs too. 'MISSY – COME NOW.'

He hoists himself up over the engine and walks dripping to where she lies. Her brow is creased so that she looks to be squinting with her eyes shut tight, and the claws are extended on her front right paw, where she has laid her head. Her tail sticks bent and stiff out behind her. Marvin breathes out. 'Missy?' he says, small. Afraid of her no answer. He touches her belly, tight and still, with the back of his fingers.

He sits himself on the top of the cooler and rests his head on her cold, faithful body and feels sadness in his nose and eyes, and he circles her with his arms above his head and wants to draw her in. He always wanted to hold her more, like this, but she didn't much like it. She used to squirm a little. She preferred a muss of her coat or a pat on the head, or best, a nudge beneath her chin. But now he holds her like he wanted to, like he loves her.

'Marv? Missy die?' Marvin doesn't move, just circles her tighter.

'Marvin, that's a shame.'

Memories of Missy swim around in Marvin's head and together they all point at him and his sadness. He thinks of other reasons why he is sad, and Missy's little stiff frame becomes them all. He cannot imagine any life of his not punctuated by her. He smells her doggy smell, breathes it right in, fills up his lungs with thoughts of her.

And then he sits up. 'Sion, take us to Haggerty's Cove.'

He takes off his long, shiny red vest, lays it flat on the front deck and places her gently on it. He tries to smooth out the worry creases above her eyes with his thumb but they are set. He wraps the vest around her and lifts her onto his lap and rides with her like that through the rough sea, the boat smacks down between the waves, jarring his spine and clearing his head. They reach a deep calm section offshore a wide, forested beach and Sion cuts the engine.

Marvin takes the shoulder straps of his vest and ties them tight around Missy, to hold it in place. So that a piece of him goes down with her. He stands up on the very bow of the boat and cradles her for a minute, breathing in salt air, balancing with the stem between his ankles.

He positions her on the palms of his two hands and lets her go. Buried at sea. Like she would have wanted, his sea dog.

The Roof

Juliet Trewellard

Kat leant out of the long window and looked down on the piazza below. The sun was only just up, but already swifts screamed above her head, over the red tiles of the tall hotel. Her room, hers and Alexa's, was at the very top. Below, noise reached her of people shouting. It was quite usual. They were talking, but 'Italian people always seem to shout,' Alexa had said. Why did they rise so early when they were up most of the night, it seemed? Kat could see, from up here, the tops of their heads and their strange foreshortened bodies and their hands gesticulating.

Already heat was leaking into the room. It would be another day when it was too hot to do anything but catch the little bus to the beach and lie down. Alexa was tanned nearly all over. She took off her bikini top when Mother wasn't there. Alexa's face looked cross all the time. When the parents were out of sight, she would be texting her boyfriend, Jack. Click click went the tiny buttons, buzz buzz went the reply. This went on most nights, Alexa, texting as she lay in bed, Kat trying to sleep on the bed next to her. Alexa was missing Jack, missing and missing and missing, and was angry at being forced on this holiday and away from him.

At breakfast Kat's parents were discussing a trip to Florence the next day. Alexa made a face. She was too old, she felt, to tag along with her parents. Kat, three years younger, at thirteen, knew it was best to just go along with it. It was not worth talking to Alexa who had suddenly become distant and mysterious.

Later, coming back from the beach, they felt exhausted. They seemed half blinded by the sun-glare on sand, sky and sea. In their rooms the heat seemed to seep in from the open window. The walls were hot, the sheets on the beds were hot, the towels were hot in the bathroom. Kat's tee shirt stuck to her skin. Mother fanned herself with a book. When Alexa went into their little kitchen to get a cool drink from the fridge, she cried out that she had almost burnt herself from the metal trim of the door, which was hot from the flash of sunlight which lay across it.

The parents went upstairs to lie down.

'I'm not lying down,' said Alexa. 'What do they think I am, a toddler? I'm going up to the flat roof. Coming?'

'We can't go up there, Alex.'

'Course we can. I've seen the maids go up there and tan themselves on their break. There's an iron ladder up.'

'It will be too hot at this time.'

'Why we ever came to Italy at the height of summer I'll never know. Stupid parents.'

'School holidays, no choice.'

Kat watched Alexa's long, brown leg swing over the railing. She reached the rung of the iron steps which scaled the side of the building. Her thin green skirt slid up. 'Come on,' she said.

Kat followed.

The iron ladder reached upwards. Alexa was halfway up already. Kat gripped the banister rails and had to pull hard to take her upwards. It felt precarious; her head tipped back and her hair fell at an angle behind her like a cloth. She felt the fierce white sky all around. She looked up. There was Alexa looking down at her, crouched on the flat roof, safe. Finally Kat hauled herself up beside her sister. She was out of breath.

They could feel the hot tarmacked roof through the thin soles of their beach shoes. They sat down, feeling slightly dizzy. There were red-tiled slopes around them, and looking down, they saw the small piazza spread out below, the tall houses arranged in a regular pattern around the square, with the centre fountain playing its thin sprinkle of tepid water. There was a group of boys, splashing each other noisily in the fountain. Shouts and laughter reached up to the girls and seemed to echo in the hot afternoon. No one else seemed to be about.

Alexa stood up once more.

There was a sudden whoop and a rumble of excited, incomprehensible Italian from below. The boys had noticed her. Kat stood up too. Another whoop!

'Hey – Inglesi – bellas. Come 'ere, come down a 'ere! Come – a see us!'

Alexa was grinning. It seemed as if it was the first time she had grinned that holiday. 'We're not coming down there,' she yelled.

'Che?' came up to them.

'NO!'

A large boy at the front grinned up at her. From high up they saw his flash of white teeth. 'Che cose?'

A shorter boy pushed in front of him. 'No? Then we come up!'

'Oh my God, Alex,' said Kat in a panic. But Alexa smiled.

'They are! They're coming up!'

'No! Tell them to go down, Alexa; we'll get into trouble.'

'Don't be such a wuss.'

Kat retreated from the edge and stood, uncertainly, further away. There was no other way to go as the boys were scaling the only escape route. Now the head of the short boy began to appear up over the edge of the roof.

'Ciao belle Inglese. We come up!'

His almost black hair was short and spiky. It was these spikes of hair that Kat saw first. Now she could see the gleam of his eyes. His grin was irresistible, so she grinned back. He was only a little older than her, she felt. He was short. Short and agile. He leapt onto the roof and stood up, triumphant. Four more boys quickly followed, the taller of them pushing to the front.

'God,' muttered Alexa to Kat, 'what have we let ourselves in for?' Aloud she said: 'Hello.'

‘'Allo…'allo, 'allo…’ they all chorused, giggling and joshing each other.

Alexa, in a show of sophistication, went and sat on the corner of an air vent and crossed her legs. The boys followed, circling around like greedy starlings. Kat was left standing, looking on. The big boy, who sat down next to Alexa, shuffled nearer. He looked up at the smaller boy with spiky hair and said something.

‘'E say 'e larve you,’ translated the short boy, and as he grinned, he looked over to Kat and winked.

‘Si,’ said the tall boy. He made an effort. ‘Si, I larrrve you. You larrrve me, si? Bella, bellissima, si. Kees me?’

Alexa, calm, lifted her mouth to his.

‘Alex!’ Kat said, but Alexa smiled a slow smile and let her lips come close to the boy. They kissed, rather clumsily and briefly, but all the boys around cheered. Kat cautiously moved closer. The boys made way for her, indicating, with exaggerated and flamboyant courtesy, a seat on the air vent next to Alexa.

The shorter boy pushed in next to her, grinning. His black hair looked shot with blue in the bright light. Kat felt a pang at the beauty of it, but she also noted, with quick disdain, his dirty fingernails.

‘Come, little one,’ he said. ‘You kees me, like them?’

‘No,’ said Kat.

‘Oh,’ he moaned, in mock dejection, ‘I bleeding, my 'eart is bleeding.’ The rest of the boys were grinning, but not comprehending. He turned to them and translated, doing an elaborate mime of a wounded lover, suffering from heartache. The boys screeched with laughter. He turned back to Kat. ‘You no like me to bleed to death, no? So just a leetle kissy for me, no?’

Almost against her will she leant in to him and he touched her lips with his. Then he grinned at her. The surrounding boys whooped some more. Alexa was snogging the big boy but now she pulled away and stood up, smiling calmly.

'We have to go now,' she said and, as if in awe of her, they all parted and let her walk to the edge of the roof and start to climb down. 'Come on Kat,' she ordered.

'Cat? A leetle cat?' asked the spiky-haired boy. He turned to the others. 'Gattino,' he said and they laughed. 'My leetle kitten,' he said to her. 'Tonight? 'E wants to see you. We all want to see you.'

'We can't tonight,' said Alexa.

'Tomorrow? Up 'ere? You too, kitten?'

Kat looked at him, 'Come ON!' said Alexa.

They eased themselves down from the rungs of the ladder to their balcony and crept into their bedroom. There was no sound from next door.

Alexa fixed her eye on Kat, who was breathless and had her mouth slightly open. 'You fool,' she said, dismissively.

Kat sat down. The spiky-haired boy's face was still before her. His voice – 'My 'eart is bleeding,' – went around her head. 'Are we going tomorrow?' she asked Alexa.

'I haven't made up my mind yet,' Alexa said.

***

'The worst possible temperature for walking around museums,' grumbled Alexa. 'If they point out one more marvel I shall scream.' But even she couldn't help be somewhat impressed. As for the long spaces of the Uffizi, and the huge paintings that surrounded them, a sort of hush descended upon them all, and even the heat was forgotten. Kat wandered round on her own. She felt dizzy, as if she were still on the roof. Before her were these brilliant colours – a deep blue, a gold, a bright red of a jacket beneath the proud face of a Medici prince. Father talked of the blood line. He talked of the passion of the Renaissance spirit. Kat saw a young Botticelli male who looked suddenly like the boy who wanted to kiss her. She saw pictures of battles, bodies bleeding with spear wounds. She saw a painting of Judith and the severed head of Holofernes. There was blood running down the woman's arm.

She was quiet on the drive home. That night, after dinner at the restaurant, Alexa moved close beside her as the family walked back. 'Let's go up on the roof as soon as Mum and Dad have gone to bed,' she whispered.

The dark evening seemed as hot as day. They wore their thin tee shirts and skirts. They sat near the edge of the shadowed roof and waited. What were they waiting for? Alexa said nothing, yet Kat knew. All around them the sky unfurled its splendour, and Kat gazed upwards, looking up at the stars, then down again, to the ground far below.

Then they saw them, the boys, coming across the square. They were coming! Somewhere a dog started to howl. Distant music reached them, its bass beat thudding. Kat and Alexa watched the group of boys as they moved across the square – the jerky movements, the bumping into each other, the quick shouts of laughter, the gabble of their voices coming up to them. Now they made out the tall one ('Alexa's', Kat thought) and then behind him they saw the short one ('mine') with the spiky hair. As she made out the gleam of his teeth, he looked up, raising his hand.

Suddenly, the group turned and scattered and then came together again in a tense huddle. Why? Kat then turned her head a little and saw, from around a corner, another group of boys. Alexa shifted beside her and touched her arm. They heard the second group's voices shouting out harshly, jeering and as they watched they saw the dark bend of their shoulders and the quickened movements of their feet. At the front there was a large boy with a bright green top which caught the light like a flag.

The two girls watched, transfixed. Before they realised what had happened, Kat and Alexa saw a boy leap on another. They saw a boy fall to the floor and then jump up again quickly. Then, in a moment, though they could scarcely believe it, they watched a furious fight break out amongst them all.

'What shall we do, Alex?' said Kat in an urgent whisper. 'We must tell someone.'

'We can't, we can't! Wait, maybe it will settle down.'

They both stood now, staring at the scene below.

No one seemed to hear the fight but the girls, and the distant dog that started barking furiously, answered by another dog. The boys continued scrambling, as in a rough dance. Suddenly there came a huge shout, a kind of cry. The boys started apart, then three of the rival gang turned and ran off, calling to the others. Two stayed, bent over something then moved out. Then Kat saw the boy with the spiky hair stagger and lean against the tall boy and before she could make sense of it, something in her seemed to burst and she heard herself give a quick little gasp.

'Where are you going?' hissed Alexa, but it was too late – Kat had run to the ladder.

'Come back you idiot,' Kat heard her sister call, but already she was halfway down, one foot feeling for the rung and quickly replacing it with the next, on, on, down to the ground.

When she reached the last rung, she jumped and ran out into the square. Without thinking, she was rushing across the cobbles, her shadow, from the street lights, making short, dark streaks as she ran. She neared the boy with the spiky hair and he saw her. She caught the white flash of his eye and saw his mouth open. He was rubbing the side of his belly with one hand, and he lurched a little towards her.

'Back, back! Go back!' he called and ran, in a crooked, limping way to meet her. He pushed her. 'Go back!' But the boy in the green top was beside him in a moment, his arm moving in a thrust. Kat found herself shoved aside. She felt the short boy's shoulder beside her, then a peculiar jolt as his body fell against her and slid downwards. Now the air was shocked with harsh yells and the boys' feet were thudding away. She saw the bright green of the big boy's top flare up like neon as he passed the light of the hotel.

She stood for a moment watching them run. Then she looked down. The boy – her boy, the boy with the spiky hair, the boy who called her Gattino, little kitten – lay on the ground, crooked on the cobbles, as if thrown there.

Kat bent down. As she did he raised his head and whispered to her. But his English deserted him, and though she got close to his face, she couldn't understand what he said. It seemed as if he said something urgent, something vital and she leant over him again to try and understand what it was. The boy reached out to her and touched her. She felt something wet and saw, even in the half-light of lamps, a shine of vivid red! She had blood on her hand! She stood up, her heart thumping.

She knew she must help him. But suddenly – a shudder, and the wail of police sirens pierced the dark street and the distant dog started barking once more. But before the police arrived, out from between the corners of the buildings, out from the shadows, boys rushed. They pushed past Kat and picked up the boy, running off with him, awkwardly carrying him as if a heavy burden. Kat heard him groan.

'Don't move him!' she cried. By now Alexa had climbed down, but the boys were hurrying away. Kat saw 'her' boy's arm bump along the road. 'Don't – you'll …' She took one or two steps after them and then saw little dots of blood following them as a trail.

The police sirens howled nearer and nearer.

'Quick!' cried Alexa. But Kat was standing and staring so Alexa grabbed her arm and roughly pulled her.

The girls ran towards the back of the hotel, just as the van burst into the square.

Now the hotel was lit up, rectangles of yellow light at the windows. They heard the front door open and a man's voice gabbling. Then a few words they recognised: '…Signorine Inglese…'

'Don't say a word about anything!' hissed Alexa as they ran up the back stairs and into their room.

The hotel was noisy with voices, people shouting in the corridors. Their bedroom door opened. Mother, in her long thin wrap, stood in the square of light.

'I thought you'd have been woken by the racket,' she said, coming nearer. 'Nothing to worry about – a fight among local youth gangs. One boy was hurt, it seems. It's all over now; not to worry, darlings. Go back to sleep.' She went out and shut the door.

Kat lay back on the bed and stared at the ceiling. Then she turned her head and looked at Alexa. 'Phew!' she said. 'We're alright, Kat, the police won't come here now. It's over.'

Kat stared at her. Then she watched Alexa turn over and settle in her bed. Kat lay there, listening. After a bit the noise quietened down and eventually she heard the police van speed off, its siren on again.

***

The next morning, in the bathroom, Kat found blood between her legs.

'It's your period stupid,' said Alexa. 'Don't you know anything?'

Yes, yes, of course. But – the colour, the boy, the blood. Perhaps, indeed, she didn't know anything.

Making the long journey back to England, two days later, Alexa dozed to the hum and steady rhythm of the car, but Kat couldn't sleep. She had a new dull ache in her stomach. She had a new dull ache in her heart. The pictures from the Uffizi drifted by, one after the other, in her head – the brilliant colours, the disturbing faces. Mingled with these was the face of the boy, the boy who bled on her, the boy who tried to make her understand.

Kat thought of the blood between her legs which she must get used to every month. She thought of the little spots of blood on the cobbles as the boy was carried away. What if he had died? She felt her inside lurch and a stab of pain, the new pain. Why did she feel guilty? She couldn't understand what the boy had said, could she? She couldn't understand.

Short Pants
James Lawless

Tar melted on roadways that summer, sticking to car tyres and bicycle tyres and the rubber soles of children's runners. The furze burned on the mountain. The burning, some was handmade, the rest was an act of god or whatever. The bigger boys liked to spark the sulphur to supplant the coconut smell of the furze's yellow florets with the smell of scorching, just to see how it would go down.

The ferns grew high that summer, as high as my five foot four. We played in the fields which shimmered with their soft green fronds, and became transformed with the long evenings from short to tall (Mam said I grew two inches at the end of that summer), from pale to tan, from thin to brawn. We were nurtured by the sea air, the sun, the heat and the fresh lettuces and tomatoes purchased from the local farms. They were all weaning us away from childlike ways and carrying us forward into an unsure region. The ferns took on a different feel that summer; I became conscious of something, a different meaning in things. The green sea of change, places for hiding, the sandy hollows, the insects we were familiar with; they were part of us; the sound of crickets, caterpillars with their larvae hatching unimpeded on the fronds; the delight of the soft camouflage (unlike the prickliness of furze) for animal and insect, for cowboys and Indians with moving feathers; just the tops of the feathers could be seen traversing as if self-propelled through the ferns; and the bows with rubber suctioned arrows sailed through the air. The smell from the caps of the *pistoleros*; the jungle hunger; rabbits on the run. That's the way it was every summer, sometimes the fronds dripping with rain or dew – we didn't mind. But this summer was hotter and more sultry than any previous one I could recall. 'Overpowering,' Mam said. And the ferns became charged with new discoveries, new secrets, rendezvous with deeper substance now, imaginary twilight trysts with Elizabeth.

She was three years older than me. Fifteen. A jouncer, flaunting her maturity at the young boys of the area as she undulated in her blue jeans through the ferns like the apparition of a goddess. We remained crouched in a freezeframe waiting for ambush, guns and bows at the ready. Ah yes, Elizabeth spoiled our game plan; she rode roughshod over us. And there was no one to shout, 'Go away, girl,' for we, like the caterpillars, were at the point of turning.

We were at the point of turning (except for my younger brother of course and his immature pals who didn't even notice Elizabeth and were still shrieking Indians). We stared in silent awe, our weapons hanging impotently by our sides, as she shimmied down the dirt track. Her swim towel was draped fancy-free over her shoulder, swaying in rhythm with the music of her body, sending out messages though all the secret pathways of the ferns. She drew us in her wake (the feathers moving swiftly with greater urgency now; up periscopes through the sea of green). We observed the pubescent curves of her which, speaking with their lateral swagger, were saying, Ah you boys, you admirers, I can see you; I have radar in the back of my head specially to pick out little predatory males with their salivating mouths, ogling me. Oh, and she smiled knowingly with that half turn: I have something you desire, a thing of mystery for you boys in your pencil straightness.

Elizabeth: she shared with five sisters (no brother, alas, whose brains I could have tapped for the secrets). They were staying in a converted tram two fields away from our converted train carriage. Her tram with the bell still functioning. It was a pleasure any time I called to ring that bell with its little hammer action and say – to the yawns of the girls on board – 'Fares please'. 'Little boys have to have their fun,' Elizabeth eventually said, and I never rang the bell again after she said that.

We played croquet on their smooth stretch of grass; that's when she said, buttering up to me I thought, 'You have a lovely tan on your legs, Jamie.' I had as good a tan, as it happened, on my arms, being of a sallow complexion, but she never mentioned them. Then continuing to scan upwards, she said, 'And your little short pants.' At this, herself and her sisters burst into a titter. I blushed; the comment was so pointed, so sexual, and yet at the time I did not quite know it was sexual; but it was the tone, the mocking tone of its delivery.

I became self conscious and very aware of my appearance after that sweltering day in the croquet field. I can't even remember who I was with at the time, but those I was with, the other boys I mean, were every bit as bewildered as I was. There was none of that customary puerile slagging we reserved for lesser mortals; rather heads were cast down in homage as it were to the skygoddess who had spoken. And all I could do was dwell silently on the ignominy of short pants.

The heat was so intense that I was not able to sleep that night. I tossed and turned in my bed, the sheets becoming moist with my sweat. It was like I was coming down with a fever. I lay in the top bunk, having drawn the long straw over my younger brother for that privilege (I couldn't confide in him about my feelings, being as he was at a totally asexual stage). I gazed through the carriage window at a full moon shining; it was so strong the light, like a day – another excuse I convinced myself for my insomnia. But I knew it wasn't really the moon or the heat that were the causes of my discomfort. It was Elizabeth. The blonde, blue-eyed goddess whose words cast people down. A queen of Sheba, a Delilah, a scheming Cleopatra with the milk-soft skin. Elizabeth was all of those. And the moon shifted, lighting up the short pants draped over the frame at the end of the bed: the fawn cotton with the brown leather belt and steer's head buckle, which my brother coveted, so childishly.

I told Mam next morning that I wanted long pants.

'What would you be wearing long pants for in this heat?' she said. 'Let the sun at your legs.'

'I get cuts,' I lied.

'Where?' she said, examining me, 'I don't see any cuts. You haven't been up in the furze, have you?'

'No, Mam.'

'I told you not to go up there, with all the fires.'

'I want jeans,' I shouted, 'blue jeans.'

'What's wrong with you, Jamie?' she said. 'Why are you shouting?'

'You wouldn't have a clue,' I shouted again and stomped off.

I felt bad about annoying Mam; she hadn't been well lately and had to stay indoors on doctor's orders. She loved nothing better than to sit on her khaki-coloured deckchair outside the carriage door with her Daphne Du Maurier or Catherine Cookson to entertain her. And she'd read like that, the sun dappling her wan face. At mealtimes she'd blow her silver whistle which she wore on a lanyard around her neck to call us in from the fields. And we'd come with a whelp, my brother and I and any visiting cousins, running through the ferns, trooping into the sun window where the table was set.

But lately I started chewing on other things besides food, musing to myself. 'Eat up your salad, Jamie,' Mam said. 'I'm not hungry,' I said. 'He's in love,' my brother taunted. 'Shut up, you,' I said. 'What would you know?' And then I'd start imagining our train carriage was slipping its mooring and taking off from the field. It would pull into a station, and there on the platform would be Elizabeth waiting for me in her blue jeans, but with that laugh, that semi-smirk, distorting the beauty of her lightly freckled face.

Some thoughts cast long shadows. Why was Mam staying indoors and taking to the bed quietly, furtively almost, in the afternoons when all the washing-up was done? Why was she seizing those moments for herself? She never explained. She just said Dr Eppel had told her that it would only be for a short while to get her temperature down. 'What temperature?' I said with alarm in my voice. 'The heat,' she said. 'Nothing to worry about.' Dr Eppel didn't want her to come by the sea that summer, but she wouldn't miss it, not for her boys who looked forward to their sunshine and sea air every year, and tasted freedom for a while in the wide open spaces before returning to the grime and restrictions of city living. 'We'll be back in the flat world for long enough,' Mam said. She hadn't recovered from Dad's death last winter. The suddenness of his going numbed us. 'We'll be needing the sun now to thaw us out,' Mam said, but she was more numbed than me or my brother. Dr Eppel had put her on an iron tonic because she looked so pale. We youngsters had things to entertain us, but Mam was a solitary creature at the best of times. Although she liked kids and encouraged cousins to visit, she was as happy with a book as with any adult companion. 'A book won't talk back to you,' she'd say, trying to maintain a cheerful outlook for our sakes, but I knew Dad's ghost was haunting her. Even his old navy dungarees hanging on a hook near the front door of the carriage, she refused to throw out. I knew she was pining away on her own those sultry afternoons, when my brother and I were lost in the ferns and all the washing-up was done. But I didn't over-dwell on such matters, my mind being suffused as it was with Elizabeth. More than anything in the world, during those hot summer days, I longed to touch her; it was a burning desire, like the furze burning on the mountain; I wanted to taste her cherry lips to ascertain that she was flesh and blood, and not some blue sky deity.

She went to a hop the evening after my sleepless night – to Mr Thomas's converted hut. The bigger and older boys of course would be going; they would be able to dance with her, to hold her hand, to walk her home. I would not be allowed to go to such a place. 'Plenty of time,' Mam would say to my mild enquiry, 'plenty of time for things like that.'

I was beginning to panic. When was I going to stretch, to grow taller? Was it ever going to happen? And short pants. Who ever heard of someone going to a hop in short pants?

Elizabeth smiled at me going down the dirt track.

'Bye-bye, short pants,' she said, and she swished past in a flow of yellow summer dress like a turning sunflower, the sweet scent of her perfume, wafting on the evening air. It drew me from my crouched position among the ferns. I had been waiting there in a half-hearted pose of ambush for so long that I was indifferent to detection. I emerged to the distant cry of my brother: 'Where are you going? That's not fair.' I followed her down the dirt track at the end of which she met a group of the bigger fellows and girls all dolled-up.

'Beat it, kid,' a tall fellow shouted at me, hunting me away as if I were a stray dog. And Elizabeth turned around with a look of pretended surprise that I had been following her. 'Back to Mammy,' she said, 'before it gets dark.' And with a peal of laughter, they walked on.

I slouched home. I didn't wait for Mam's whistle – the call before dark. The sky still carried slivers of light through its growing inkiness. My brother would be out there yet among the warrens of ferns, wallowing with his pals in their childish softness. The air was balmy, ever carrying, I imagined, the fragrance of Elizabeth's perfume, intoxicating, unlike those stupid ferns which had no scent at all.

I returned to the train carriage and looked at Dad's old dungarees hanging on their hook. I took them down and changed into them, turning the legs up a bit to accustom myself to their bagginess. Mam was resting in her bedroom with her transistor radio playing. She did not hear me coming in and going out again with my short pants in my hands.

I looked towards the mountain: the furze was burning, lighting up the night with an orange glow. Drawn towards it, I could smell the scorching and hear the crinkling of the blackened earth. I placed the pants on a thorn of blaze and watched them. There was a hesitancy as if the bush were unsure whether to return the product as unsuitable or not. But slowly a flicker took hold, and the pants darkened in unison with the earth. I had removed the belt with the steer's head to bestow later on my brother. At least, I thought, that would be worth a few favours in times to come.

Shit Happens

Laurie Porter

So here we are, newly wed, in the dry winter African veld with its grass-dust expanse of straw yellow. We come here because you need an open space to fly your model planes.

There is no sign of life but across the field we can make out angular grey shapes – stacked sheets of corrugated tin – a squatter camp. We know there are people crammed in those makeshift houses but we hear and see no one. It suits us this way.

You fly your plane while I sit and watch. The winter sun is pleasant and I feel sleepy and content. You stop for a sandwich and we pour coffee from a flask and sip from a shared cup.

'Another hour?' you suggest and I smile sleepily. I love being with you.

I doze while you fly then I become chilled as the mid-afternoon temperature drops. You land the plane, wipe it down and start to pack up. The boot of the Chevy is open as you put things away. I stand and shake the dry grass and sand from the blanket, fold it and put it on the back seat.

Then this dog appears. Its huddled shape crawls around the edge of the field. It gets as close as it dares and we see it's sandy brown and its hair would be silky if it wasn't so matted. I guess it's a young bitch but we can't tell the breed. It skulks around us, its tail curled tightly between unsteady legs. Its ribs press drum-taut through patchy fur and the ears are well back and trembling. I suppose it's looking for something to eat. It looks as if it's never been well cared for. Any movement makes it start and it skitters on the tips of its feet, ready to scuttle away. Its infected eyes look at us for brief nervous moments then back down at the ground. Flies follow it hungrily and when they land on its back, its skin shivers them off.

'Poor thing,' I say.

You look at me and you read me. You tilt your head reproachfully.

'Don't even think about it,' you warn, 'it's not coming home with us. It belongs to someone. We can't just take it.'

You are always the sensible one.

'It's neglected,' I say, 'No one would notice it's gone…'

You call me sentimental and stalk away not wanting to be part of this. You hide your head in the boot of the car and busy yourself with your things.

I crouch and set about befriending the animal. I talk reassuringly to coax it to me. I hold out my hand, pretending I have food for it. It takes a few steps forward then prances back uncertainly. Slowly, slowly I win its confidence until it's standing near enough to touch. I offer it the back of my hand and it sniffs. I wait and wait. Eventually it lets me touch it. The top of its head is stiff with knotted hair and the skin underneath is scabby.

You lurk in the background pretending not to notice.

When I pick it up it struggles a little but makes no sound. It wriggles into the footwell of the front passenger seat and falls in an awkward heap. Pulling the door to, against my body, I stretch back and get the blanket to cover the dog. I climb in, my hand still holding the dog down, and struggle to pull the door closed. You get into the driver's seat and shake your head. You start the engine. The dog is trembling. I stroke its head and talk to it soothingly. I try out names.

You look straight ahead and say, 'I don't know what you think we're going to do with it.'

I say, 'We couldn't just leave it there.'

You say, 'Well, we can't keep it.'

'I know,' I say.

'We can't keep it,' you say again, 'you know we're not allowed pets in the flat.'

I don't answer.

Once you've parked the car, you get out and slam the door. I drape the dog with the blanket so it's completely covered. I clamber out, then reach in and pick the dog up. It is not heavy but it squirms awkwardly. I kick the car door shut behind me. You lock the car and walk ahead of me towards the stairs. I'm fighting to keep the dog covered and hoping that no one will see us. You fling open the front door to our flat and go inside. When I get there you're hanging up your coat. I put the dog down gently and pull the blanket off it. It stands, its back legs shuddering. Then it shits all over the parquet floor.

'Great,' you say, 'dysentery.'

'It isn't dysentery,' I say and I pick the dog up by its front legs and drag it spread-legged into the bathroom. The shit slithers down its fur and leaves a trail on the floor.

It yelps as I lift it into the bath. It tries to scrabble out, its claws scratching on the enamel. 'Just stay there!' I yell at it, 'Stay!' and it cowers low in the bath, but it stays – trembling – and watches me walk from the room.

'Oh, so now you're an expert on dysentery?' Your voice is echoing from the kitchen cupboard where you're rummaging. You bring me a roll of paper towel, disinfectant spray and a plastic bag from OK Bazaars.

'Yes.'

I snatch the towel, rip off some squares, crouch in front of the mess and lay a circle of towel around the slime. I wipe inwards and upwards trying to scoop up the shit.

I say, 'I'll tell you what dysentery is. Dysentery is when you eat a handful of raw runner beans when you're home from boarding school one weekend. And then Monday morning you're standing in assembly and your skin goes clammy and there's a high-pitched ringing in your ears then it all goes black and you can't remember anything 'til you wake up in the sanatorium. And you're lying curled up tightly because the stomach cramps are tearing your insides apart...'

I rip off more towel and lay it on top of the shit, watch the brown as it soaks in, watch it slowly spreading. The patch spreads so quickly and so wide. I am amazed.

'...and you have the shits so badly that it comes out like burning water hundreds of times a day and you worry each time that you're not going to make it to the bog. And when you go everything explodes in the bowl and the shit has blood and mucus in it and the stomach cramps don't go away. And Nurse has to look at your stools so you ring the bell and you hear her clomp down the corridor to the bathroom. You hear her spraying air freshener before she bustles back to you and shovels another dose of kaolin down you...'

I scoop up the stinking, sodden mass and you hold the bag open for me. You look away as the bunch of towels drop in. You have to look away – you cannot bear things like this. I see the translucent white of the plastic bag as it smears brown inside. The stench is making me gag but I just want to get it over and done with.

'You okay?' you ask. I ignore you and take another swipe at the floor. On all fours I follow the trail to the bathroom door, flooding the floor with disinfectant squirts and wiping, and wiping and wiping. You shuffle along with the bag collecting the saturated wadges of paper.

'...and you think that, seeing as you're this ill, your mother will come and get you and take you home. But she doesn't. It's different for the parents who live in Zambia or Malawi but your mother lives only fifteen minutes away...'

I use up the last of the paper towel to soak up the disinfectant and throw the pieces into the bag. You tie the bag shut and take it outside the front door. You shut the door and turn to look at me.

'*This* isn't dysentery.' I realise I'm shouting. Your eyebrows are raised in bewilderment and I feel a rush of shame. I look away giving you the reprieve you're after. We're still too new for this.

There's a pause, then you say, 'Well, it's got to go. We can't keep it.'

The floor of our rented flat is stained white where the shit was and I agree. We can't keep the dog.

I shower the dog, massage shampoo into it and the dirt pours off in gritty foam. The wet fur lays pasted flat on its skinny frame except where the knots won't release. The scabs all over its body stand proud. You pass me a towel and I dry. I start with its ears and its head. It shuts its eyes as I smear the muck away from them. I rub gently down its sides, around its ribs and under its belly. It's still shivering and I lift it from the bath. You lay a blanket in the corner and I put the dog there, pushing it to lie down. It watches me all the time and when it's lying, its tail wags – two thumps. I stroke the dog's muzzle and tell it to be good. We put newspaper all over the floor, give the dog some water and shut it in for the night. It doesn't mess the floor overnight and I'm glad because it means I was right about the dysentery.

The next day we conceal the dog in its blanket and sneak down to the car. We're laughing and you say I'm mad and how did you ever get hitched to someone like me? We put lots of towels on the floor of the car and lay the dog on top and we drive to my mother's house.

'So we just turn up at your mother's, tell her we stole a dog, that it's ill and she has to look after it?'

'Of course not,' I say, 'She'll make us take it back.'

We get out of the car leaving the dog there. I say to my mother that there's this dog and how awful it was because we found it wandering on the highway. It was running scared between the cars and nearly got killed; and that we managed to catch it on the central reservation and that we don't know what to do with it now. We'd keep it if we could.

She says she can't believe how cruel people can be. She says how lucky it was we were there. She says she'll keep the dog.

She comes to the car. You pass her the blanket and she watches as I get the dog out. It hangs its head and looks at her through watering eyes as I carry it to the house. Its tail wags weakly a couple of times. She strokes it as we walk inside. She lays the blanket on the floor of the living room and I put the dog on top of it. It stands there looking at us.

'Lie down,' I tell it but it stays standing on the blanket. 'Lie down.' But it just looks at me. It's getting on my nerves now.

I see my mother watching.

'It might have diarrhoea,' I say and she says that's okay because she'll get it to a vet to be checked anyhow. She makes tea and puts biscuits on a plate and we drink and talk. The dog sits and watches us. After a while I notice it is lying down and we forget that it's there until we get up to leave.

'Thanks,' I say to my mother. She says that's okay. She says she won't come to see us off – she thinks she should stay with the dog. As we walk out the door she is straightening out the blanket. She is patting the dog and talking to it. She's telling it that she's going to look after it and that it will get better.

You start the car and we drive off. I struggle with tears that are fighting for control. You look over at me and say, 'You're such a softy, aren't you?'

I look out of the window as the veld flies past in a blur. Hot tears sting my face.

'Hey.' You reach over and squeeze my arm. We can't pull over because we're already on the highway.

'It will be alright,' you say.

'Yes,' I say, 'I suppose it will.'

Brief Lives

Editor: Susan Tranter

Saint Francis of the Dead Birds

David Bateman

With the unofficial canonisation of the so-called 'Saint Francis of the Dead Birds' now more or less acknowledged by the Church, it is probably only a matter of time before official beatification follows. The unvanquishable faith, the goodwill and the good works of Francesco of Torino have scarcely been in doubt; and nor has the fact of the associated miracles. Rather it is the cruelty of these miracles which the Church has found so hard to live with: a grotesque cruelty that the Church now struggles to face and to rise above – the very same task that Francesco Fortini of Torino himself faced every day of his adult life.

The nature of these miracles is only too easy to define: that is, that at certain times, any bird flying directly over him would spontaneously, and with no other cause, fall immediately dead to the ground. Mere height was no protection from this effect, though birds flying even a single metre horizontally away from him would be entirely unharmed; thus wherever Francesco was upon the globe, there would effectively be a towering vertical column above him – invisible, intangible, yet within which no bird could survive.

Just as there are those who, in their support for Francesco's beatification, prefer to acknowledge his miraculous qualities whilst ignoring the fundamentally unpleasant nature of these miracles, there are a few people who, for their own reasons, like to see Francesco's life as nothing more than a continual wholesale slaughter. This idea of a constant avian bloodbath is firmly contradicted by three observations on the established facts of Francesco's life.

In the first place, these deaths never occurred until he was in his mid-teens: the first witnessed instance occurred when he was fifteen. In the second place, the quality seems to have at first occurred only occasionally and momentarily; the second such event to be witnessed by others did not occur until he was nearly eighteen. And in the third place, the quality was only ever intermittent throughout his life, and there are records of countless occasions on which flocks of birds flew over him entirely unscathed.

On the other side, there are those who claim that Francesco not only talked with birds, but also apologised individually to every single bird whose death he caused. Though this is almost true, it is an unworthy attempt to place Francesco on a level with his saintly predecessor of Assisi, and does Francesco Fortini no favours by refusing to acknowledge the facts. True, Francesco Fortini did talk to birds, and did apologise to those which fell dead beside him. But he himself never claimed to have spoken to every bird that died thus, and several times stated the sheer impossibility of even noticing the death of every such bird. Doubtless there were countless birds of which he was unaware, dying unnoticed on the rooftops of buildings in which he had spent but a few minutes.

The comparison with Saint Francis of Assisi, admittedly inevitable, has always been a regrettable one, since so many elements of Francesco's life can be presented as a cruel parody of his saintly predecessor – a fact not lost upon the detractors of the more recent Francis, including a number of newspaper cartoonists at the time when the possibility of his beatification was first mooted, a few years after his death. But even the briefest of accounts of the key events of his life show us that here was a man struggling to find the best use for himself in the larger scheme of things.

Orphaned by World War Two, Francesco was brought up in a children's home in Torino, and had always been a quiet, thoughtful child – one who was unlikely to take in his stride the events that would so shortly assail him. As a sensitive teenager, he was deeply upset by the deaths of birds around him, and by his own account, it was when he was sixteen that he began apologising to each bird that fell dead by him. He was frequently heard apologising to birds in general, and would often shout out in warning to individual birds if he happened to notice them flying towards him.

It is important to remember that since the death of a bird flying over him when he was fifteen, no one else witnessed another such incident until he was nearly eighteen. Consequently, his habit of talking to birds was regarded by those who knew him as a deranged overreaction to an unfortunate chance event in his past, and as a sign of incipient mental instability. Fortunately his work was based entirely indoors – he began as an apprentice engineer for Fiat during this time – but even so, he could not utterly avoid having to go outside sometimes in his life. His shouting at birds, which obviously attracted attention, was usually taken by strangers to indicate some sort of phobia – an interpretation he could probably have lived with – but whenever he attempted to explain himself to acquaintances, he was invariably regarded as suffering from delusions.

This inevitably led to Francesco's first encounters with the psychiatric profession, which in turn led, again inevitably, to a diagnosis of paranoid schizophrenia, which at that time was even more of a catch-all designation than it is today.

His first spell in psychiatric care – the only time that he refused to be admitted voluntarily – came when he was eighteen. Ironically, this was only months after the second witnessed instance of a bird dropping dead while flying over him – an event dismissed at the time as a deeply unfortunate coincidence.

His treatment reaching an obvious impasse, Francesco was discharged and returned to his work at Fiat, where for nearly another year he was the butt of his workmates' jokes. The discovery of a number of dead birds on the roof of his sector of the Fiat works changed this. He was briefly suspected of having deliberately killed them and placed them there so as to support his delusion. But within a month of this, when two starlings fell dead on the ground behind Francesco within seconds of each other as he was leaving work, the event was witnessed clearly by over a dozen Fiat employees.

Francesco's life entered a new phase. For other people, he had now become a bizarre physical phenomenon rather than a psychiatric case; and Francesco himself gave many accounts of the relief he felt now that he was believed at last. But this relief was offset by a deepening of the original trauma. For it was all too clear to Francesco – as well as to others – that the reason the phenomenon was now more conspicuous was that 'the Francesco effect' – as some papers had dubbed it – was now occurring with greater frequency and persisting for longer periods.

The constant knowledge of the piling up of dead birds on the roof over his head eventually undermined Francesco's ability to face staying in any one place, and at twenty he gave up his engineering job to become a driver. There is certainly an arguable truth in his belief that by being so much on the move in a large, noisy lorry, he was actually passing under far fewer birds than would have passed over him had he stayed in his earlier, more static job. But Francesco himself later suggested that probably his main motivation was simply an attempt to run away: to escape seeing the consequences of his terrible miracle.

This period of his life was to end in tragedy, a tragedy for which he himself always insisted on taking the blame, though a direct link was never established. What was certain, though, was that about one minute after Francesco had passed along a particular stretch of autostrada near La Spezia, a lorry travelling along the same carriageway behind him suddenly lost control and crashed into the central barrier, causing a pile-up of fourteen vehicles and resulting in two deaths including that of the lorry driver, in whose cab a dead seagull was found.

When he learned of the accident through the radio news that same evening, the effect upon Francesco was extreme. He gave up his driving job the following day, and a week later was admitted as a voluntary in-patient at the same psychiatric hospital in Torino to which he had been mistakenly committed some six years earlier. Francesco always described this as a time of despair, frankly confessing his belief that if he had not been admitted to the hospital, he would almost certainly have killed himself so as to rid the world of a liability. But it was also at this time that he began to find some comfort in his religion, and in particular the possibility of the truth of the bible's statement that not one sparrow falls except with God's knowledge and consent; and by implication – if we are to believe in God's goodness – with some purpose.

The next part of Francesco's story is painful to tell, for the way in which he initially sought this purpose was undeniably crass, even cruel; but there is no denying that it sprang from his Christian beliefs. Also, we must remember that this was a man who, still seeing himself as less than worthless, and now also over-identifying himself with his particular, catastrophic 'talent', was desperately trying to find some way – indeed, *any* way – in which he could be of some use to society and humankind. His desperation is perhaps emphasised by the fact that he was still being treated for clinical depression through much of this time, and was twice admitted for brief periods as a psychiatric in-patient.

Enough of excuses. It is important to let Francesco's life speak for itself. But the fact is, his new work was not pretty. Essentially, he was hired by town and city authorities to work as a street-cleaner in those urban areas particularly afflicted by over-population of pigeons. On days when the Francesco effect occurred, pigeons would rain their deadweight forms onto the paving around him, he would scoop them into his vehicle's waste-container – apologising to each one as he did so – and the city authorities were made very happy. Not so the passers-by and tourists, who found the sight repellent. Francesco Fortini was becoming an ogre-figure, someone looked upon with shocked and slightly contemptuous awe; and he soon discovered that self-loathing can thrive as easily in menial circumstances as in tragic ones.

His next job could perhaps be seen merely as a further step along the same career path. In some of Europe's airports, there had recently been a noticeable increase in the number of crashes on take-off and aborted take-offs, all attributable to flocks of birds over the runways. Francesco's new task was to drive to and fro on the runways, bringing down the potential avian hazards. For a few months, working in Italy's more troubled airports, Francesco was able to see some honour in this, in that he was reducing a potentially life-threatening risk; but even here he began to see himself as indulging – quite literally – in overkill, in what was in fact a largely cosmetic exercise, little more than a gimmick.

So it was, then, that at the age of twenty-six, Francesco became a novice monk, placed initially at the Franciscan Friary at Chieri, just west of Torino, but soon moving to Oulx in the high Alps to the west, near the border with France. This turn to the monastic life has the outward appearance of a sudden change, but to Francesco it seems to have been a natural progression in his ongoing search for a purpose in his life, a search begun some two years earlier. He began to acknowledge again that his capacity for killing birds in flight was not his only personal quality. Though this was still not a happy time for him, he seems to have fitted in well during his four years as a novice, becoming invaluable as a mechanic and handyman not just to the monastery but also to various other community groups in the area.

He always claimed to have chosen Oulx because it was closer to the sky than most friaries, and that there would therefore be less atmosphere above him through which any birds might accidentally fly and be killed. In fact, he went to Oulx on orders; but still, it is likely that this very factor was a consideration in the decision. What is undeniable is that he spent every available opportunity for meditation high up in the mountains; and that after he had taken his holy vows, he often slept in a rough hut he had made for himself on the mountain at whose foot the friary sat.

For the next twenty years he alternated his quieter times at the friary with long spells as a famine relief worker: primarily in north-east Africa, but also elsewhere; and always as a truck-driver and mechanic. Various myths have grown up around the fact that wherever he went in areas of famine, food would occasionally come falling out of the sky. But though it is true – as Francesco himself acknowledged in his accounts – that sometimes human lives were saved by the crashing to the ground of a vulture or some other bird, he tended to dismiss its significance except as an occasional piece of good fortune.

He always maintained his preference for being as high up as possible, so that fewer birds might fly above him in danger of their lives. His Prior gently discouraged his continued habit of sleeping in his hut on the mountain, but at the same time was aware that this was Francesco's way of bearing his own particular cross as best he could. It was Francesco's way of trying to be harmless, and the Prior did not have it in him to forbid it.

Thus one autumn morning in Francesco's fifty-sixth year, when he did not return from his hut as usual, the two friars who went up to his hut found him dead there. He had frozen to death in his sleep, and the friars made a point of saying, when they came down to fetch the stretcher and assistants they would need to carry the body, that there had not been a single dead bird anywhere.

Francesco was buried there, near Oulx in the Italian Alps, rather than in his native Torino. The epitaph on his gravestone, chosen by the Prior, had always been one of Francesco's favourite quotations from the teachings of Jesus as recounted in the Gospels of Matthew and Luke. A predictable choice, perhaps, but it is hard to think of anything more appropriate than the Italian paraphrase of Jesus's own words: 'Not one sparrow falls without the Father's knowledge.'

Living with the Dead

Kathleen Jones

When I was six, we went to live in a two-room shack out the back of the funeral home. A bedroom for my mother, a bedroom for me and a lean-to made of packing cases and corrugated tin to hold the stove and an old table. We kept the milk and the frozen goods in the icebox in the mortuary. My mother had the rooms free because she cleaned for Mr Moeran who had the funeral business. I used to go with her into the chapel of rest and help her polish the caskets. Some of them were ebony black like grand pianos, and some were the polished, red wood of rich people's dining tables.

The most expensive were great satiny coffers bulging at the sides in wavy panels that held the dust, and a domed lid that had a cross in the centre with carved rays of light falling away from it right to the edge. The lid was in two sections so that you could open the top half to look at the face of the dead person. They were all lined, depending on the price, with either frilled cotton or cheap satin my mother ran up in the evenings on an old treadle machine in her room. I would hear her after I went to bed, *shrrr, shrrr, shrrr,* hour after hour; shucking the material up on the thread so the frills fell just right and then, *shrrr, shrrr, shrrr,* again, until I fell asleep.

The bathroom was through the mortuary where Mr Moeran put the stiffs out on the slab to do his vampire bit with the syringes and the tubes and the formalin, dressed up in overalls and a huge rubber apron. There was a glass case with a light inside that held all his surgical instruments. If I wanted to use the bathroom at night I had to walk through this room in the dark, but it never bothered me. Kids at school used to say, 'Isn't it kinda weird living with all those dead people?' But I never minded. They were like friends. Four or five days they were there and I got to know them real well.

One week it was old Mr Svenson, fished out of the reservoir after he went in off the bridge and they had to drag the bottom for him. His skin was green and cheesy-looking from being so long in the water. My mother had to use half a stick of Leichner to get him to look decent. His wife wanted him buried in his old felt hat and boots which Mr Moeran said was against his professional pride, all his clients being turned out real nice. But in the end he agreed to do it and let Mrs Svenson shake his powdery hand and pay him the money in instalments because the insurance hadn't come through yet.

Mr Moeran's hands were always powdery because he wore two pairs of gloves for his work and rubbed his hands in chalk dust so that the gloves would slide off and on easily. He had a white face too, with closed-in slitty eyes so that you never could tell what he was thinking.

'Born to be a mortician,' my mother said. 'Their heads are just the right shape for the top hats.'

I liked the chapel best. If you pressed a switch just inside the door, invisible organ music seeped up from behind the altar. It wasn't really an altar, just a trestle table covered with a white drape my mother laundered once a week. It had a brass cross set in the middle with brass candlesticks on either side, specially converted for electric candles. There was always a big vase of flowers in front: lilies mostly, but sometimes blue flowers, irises, delphiniums and such like, to match the carpet. A decorated script of Psalm 23 hung on the wall in a wooden frame. *Yea though I walk through the valley of death*... It had a damp stain in the top corner. When I was a kid, my mother used to tell me that it was the tears of the angels, but it was really because the roof leaked every now and then.

The caskets were placed on wooden stands in the centre of the room. If Mr Moeran wasn't there, my mother had to open them when relations came to visit. Propped up on white frilly pillows, their hair combed back, a touch of Leichner on their cheekbones to give a bit of natural colour, one hand across the chest as though they'd just dropped off for an afternoon nap, they looked very solid, very real. These weren't people who would go off in the night and not come back. You could keep them like this in the back parlour for ever. Mr Moeran used to boast that after what he did to people they'd last as long as the Egyptians. And my mother used to tell him that the prices he charged, you'd have to be an Egyptian to afford it. 'But what price immortality, Mrs Kovalski,' he'd say, winking.

The chapel felt very safe. Not like when I opened the door to the parking lot and the wind blew in. The kind of wind you knew came from a long way away and blew forever. Beyond the tarmac of the parking lot the sandy, salty scrub travelled out in every direction, so that wherever you wanted to go it would be just the same. And the sky leaned in on you, listening to all your conversations.

There's another kind of death that comes over you sometimes while you're still alive. You see things and you hear things, but they can't touch you and it's all far away, like you're watching a TV screen. The first time it happened was at school and the kids in the yard were teasing me. Ben Lomax was standing on the toes of my sneakers so I couldn't move and Randy Schultz had hold of my hair. Some of the others were jumping up and down shouting 'Ellie Kovalski has shit in her pants. Ellie Kovalski has shit in her pants.' And then – zap! Like one of those glass screens in the bank. They were still there, but they were on the other side of it. A long way away, and nothing to do with me at all.

I hated school. Sam from the gas station used to take me in the truck and then I'd sometimes get a ride back with the Range Warden. He had a gun in the back and two big Labradors, one yellow, one black. He made them ride in a mesh cage and they had little raw patches on their noses from rubbing on it. Sometimes he would put his hand on my knee and move it backwards and forwards and drive very slowly.

Mr Moeran didn't sleep with his wife. Everybody knew that. Joey at school said that his aunt had been in their house and that they had separate rooms because Mrs Moeran didn't like the smell of formalin. But when I asked Sam he said it was because she didn't like hands up her skirt that had been inside dead people. My mother didn't seem to mind. On Wednesdays Mr Moeran used to bring a six pack of beer round and stay late after I'd gone to bed. He brought me a portable TV so I could watch in my room. Once when I got up to go to the bathroom, my mother's door was open. Mr Moeran's black funeral suit and white shirt were carefully folded on a chair just inside and I could see his white legs and feet beating up and down on the end of the bed.

Joey was my friend. He lived out on the range where the railroad settlement used to be. Except there's no railroad now, only the interstate highway shooting through. Some of the old storefronts are still standing, propped up by derelict wooden buildings behind. And there are still sections of the wooden sidewalk left intact. People stare at it from the highway, but nobody comes to look. It's a bit like a museum, but no one's going to keep it like that because nothing important happened there. The place where Joey lived used to be the dry goods store, and it still had the wooden drawers and bins for corn and meal and a dry musty smell to it. His father kept the roof patched with bits of wooden shingle and he'd stuck up a big rainwater tank on a platform at the back. It wasn't much, but nobody knew who owned it any more, so they didn't have to pay rent.

Joey and his dad lived on welfare checks. His dad had a bad leg where a truck had backed over him at the depot. He had a hellish temper on account of it, and it was best to keep out of his way on the worst days. The old kerosene icebox out the back was always full of beer and bourbon. Joey used to come by our place most nights and my mother would cook him pancakes or eggs and beans, and he'd stay and watch TV for a while. He never said much, and when it was time to go he'd get up and thank my mother very politely for the food, jam his baseball cap on the back of his head and slip out of the lean-to door.

Sometimes in summer I'd go over there and we'd mess about in the old shacks. They were mostly half fallen down, the planks warped wide open, little bits of tar paper still fluttering in the draughts. When the weather got colder we broke up loose boards and lit the iron stove in the barber's shop. It was rusted almost through and glowed white, completely see-through, when it was hot. We pulled an old bench seat across the corner to keep out the prairie wind and smoked spliffs Joey got from the truck stop. They made me feel lazy and empty headed and full of silence. It was like the prairie was inside me, quietly whispering. Joey said they'd lived in five states since he could remember. His dad had worked for Amtrak. Joey said he liked the west coast best, where everything was green and lush and growing, with pine trees taller than pylons and not so much sky. He had once been taken to the sea and could still remember the smell of it and the taste of the salt. One day, he said, he'd like to go back there to live, in one of the glass-front houses built out over the bay on concrete legs, with garaging for four cars and a covered veranda. Joey wanted to be an architect. He used to draw houses in an old tattered notebook, fantasy houses with Dracula turrets, fancy staircases and swimming pools.

We spent all one summer rebuilding one of the shacks. Joey had drawn a plan of how it should be, one large room instead of three pokey cupboards, and the staircase going up in the middle all by itself. One night after we'd gone home, the roof fell in and we had to stop. 'Supposing we'd been in it when it all came down?' Joey said. We should have had scaffolding and props.

It was just after that Joey stopped coming to school. I went over to the house but it was all locked up and no one was there. My mother told me, with her funeral face on, that Joey's dad was in the police mortuary. She didn't know where Joey was. The welfare people had taken him away. I was glad they didn't bring his dad to our place. That would have been tough.

When I was sixteen and gave up going to school, Mr Moeran said he'd take me on and show me how to do 'the immortality thing'. He made it seem like a big mystery – something his father had told him, that he'd had from his father, and so on. I had to sign a bit of paper to say I'd not give any of his secrets to anyone else. He'd invented a special way of taking the inside bits of the body out invisibly, washing all the shit out of them and steeping them in preservative before they were put back. Once, we had a girl with a little three-month baby inside her and no one knew except us. It was our secret. Two funerals instead of one.

The bit I liked best was getting all dressed up in a black outfit and driving the hearse down to the cemetery. It was solemn and stately and serious and so beautiful it used to make me want to cry. Death is the most real thing there is. Dead people are much more real than the living. You can never rely on the living. Never know where you are with them.

Mr Moeran sometimes told me about the horses his father had had for the business. Two big black cross-bred horses in leather harnesses with brass buckles. They had dyed black ostrich plumes on their heads and their manes and tails were plaited with black ribbon. It used to be quite a sight, he said, watching them pull the funeral wagon with its four, black-spoked, iron-hooped, wheels. But then, when his father died and the horses got old, they were too much trouble to keep. 'Besides,' he said, 'there's not much call for that sort of thing now. Folks want it all done clean and quick.'

I can hardly remember my dad. He went off when I was four or thereabouts. Took his lunch can and went out to work one day as usual and didn't come back. We never did find out where he went. There was a rumour that he'd hitched a ride in a truck going south, but no one knew for certain. 'Could just as easily have been a freight car going north,' my mother said. She didn't waste time looking for him.

I haven't had much luck with men. Not that I haven't been dated. I could've been out every night if I'd hung out around the truck stop or the depot. But you do it once or twice and you realise they're all the same. Same beer on the breath, same sweat-smell, same turn-off. All that bumping and heaving. I never met a man I'd want to spend more than an hour with, let alone the rest of my life. Until I saw Mike.

No one had known about his heart. Weakened by a virus, they said. Everything had seemed quite normal. Guest celebrity quarterback at the local game, in possession of the ball and everyone shouting him on. And now here he was, on Mr Moeran's slab, six foot four, and a hundred and ten kilos of muscle. His name was Mike Hilliard, star player of the Denver Jets, age twenty-three, lately of the University of Austin, Texas, and the most beautiful man I had ever seen. He was cool to the touch, but not unpleasantly so, and his skin had a pale, opalescent sheen and was soft and firm at the same time. It felt good when I stroked it with my fingertips. His mother and sister came up from Houston to make arrangements to take him home with them. I had him laid out on the white satin pillows with his black hair flicked up at the sides just as it was in the photo they printed in the paper.

His mother was a Hollywood blonde wearing a skirt about ten years too short for her. She made a complete fool of herself, weeping and throwing herself all over him. Mr Moeran had to pick her off and carry her through to the office for a glass of bourbon. The sister was a ladies college type who treated me like a motel maid. She had the kind of eyes that can price your clothes at a glance and the kind of looks that make you want to go home and drown yourself. Mike lay there and ignored them both. I figured he was better off without them.

When they'd all gone, I climbed on a chair and got into the casket with him, pulling the lid down over the top of us. He smelled sweet – of formalin and hair oil. I held him close in the dark with his hair against my cheek and knew he was the only man I would ever want.

After the funeral home was closed up for the night and Mr Moeran had loaded him in the hearse ready for the trip to Houston, I packed my bag and took the keys from behind the mortuary door. I didn't know where I was going exactly, but I planned on getting some place they wouldn't find us.

There are times in your life when you want to hold everything still and not let it move on. I was never so happy as I was then, riding the blacktop with Mike. I got clean across the state before they caught up with me. Two cars pulled me over, blue lights flashing. They had me across the hood with a gun in my back, as if running off with a man was a great crime. They told me I'd got some sort of sickness with a long name. But I'm not crazy and I'm not dumb. As for Mike, his family took him back and they won't tell me where he is. Don't make no difference. Mr Moeran taught me real well. Once I'm out of here, I'll find him. Take him some flowers, talk to him. After Joey he was the only person who'd listen. As for this place, well, I ain't seen so many dead people together in the whole of my life. Just as well I'm not planning on hanging around.

True Stories and Other Tales

Crista Ermiya

My mum has never been able to tell a joke. Words are spoken in the wrong order, characters are misplaced or introduced unexpectedly, and the tone is all wrong: 'A woman finds out she has a brain tumour.' Beginnings get displaced, or are re-told, over and over: 'A man finds out he has a brain tumour. No. Start again. A man goes to the doctor.' Her endings are given away at the start: 'Or was it two men and one brain?' Even the worst joke should be a tight ball of plot, carefully unwound in a straight line with all elements in the right order, at the right time, in the right place. But my mum has never been able to tell a joke properly, and neither have I.

I have an aunt, an elder sister of my mother's, who is known amongst her family and acquaintances as a good storyteller. When she was seventeen years old, the stories began to come out of her mouth all skewed, with words and endings in the wrong places, in the wrong stories even. The doctors told my grandmother that her daughter had a brain tumour. At that time in my grandparents' fluctuating fortunes there was money (although no one can agree where it came from, whether it was theirs to spend or whether it was stolen, nor where it all went); so instead of dying, my aunt had an operation, and she lived. She was my grandmother's favourite daughter, but even Lola (which is Tagalog for grandmother) will admit that ever since she came back from the dead, my aunt has no soul. There are members of my extended family, devout Catholics, who still mention her name in their prayers for the departed.

I thought I remembered seeing a photograph of her when I was very young, sitting up in a bed with green hospital sheets and no hair, but

Mum says that can't be, there are no photographs from that time. In the photograph that doesn't exist, my aunt is smiling. She does smile, I can say truly that my aunt does smile; but she was never the same after they took out whatever had been growing in her brain, and her smile never reaches her eyes. My aunt is still a storyteller who can make a grown man set down his tools and listen, but now her stories are, more often than not, lies she makes up to suit her purpose at any given moment, and are not likely to have a happy ending for the audience. In the photograph that doesn't exist, my aunt is smiling, but her eyes are cold. She would quite possibly kill you if you have something she wants but won't part with it, and she doesn't care if you're family or not. If she were a man, I think she would have joined the army and grown rich from killing people as a mercenary soldier, and won medals for her bravery. Instead she got married, and had children, and spends her days spinning stories and gambling.

My mother is the youngest of three sisters. There were once twelve children, but six of them died, leaving only the youngest three daughters and the youngest three sons. Her sisters, Juanita and Conchita, always seemed so much older than her when she was a child. So grown-up, so glamorous. Now my mother is in her early sixties, and Tita Juanita and Tita Conchita (Tita means aunt in Tagalog) are somewhere in their seventies, and my mum says it feels like they are the same age. Tita Conchita is the storyteller. Before her brain went bad and she lost her soul, when she was a teenager and my mother was a child, she used to tell my mother stories about their mother, who was adopted, and about their grandmother, who had been adopted in her turn, and who is possibly the true beginning of our story, as far as anyone can say where the beginning is. All the stories I have about my mother's family are hand-me-downs, mis-shapen from being worn over many decades, re-told to me by my mother when I was a child, from what she can remember of Tita Conchita's stories. They may or may not be true.

This is the story of my maternal grandmother, still walking straight-backed up mountains at ninety years and counting, as told to me by my mother, many times.

This is a true story. *(She always starts like this: this is a true story.)*

Once upon a time in Hong Kong, a Spanish couple with no children were walking through the bustling streets when their attention was caught by a young girl, begging. Perhaps it was because the couple had finally accepted that they could not have children. Perhaps it was because of the beauty of the young child's face, even beneath the squalor. Whatever the reason, this couple, grown rich from sugar planting *(sometimes it's sugar, sometimes it's some other colonial enterprise)*, asked the child who she was. The child was able to tell them her name – her first name – but not who her family was, or who looked after her. She did not appear to have a home. The couple made enquiries *(of course, otherwise wouldn't it be kidnap?)* but not a single person in Hong Kong knew who this child was. So, rich and barren, they decided to take the girl with them when they went back to the Philippines. They adopted her and brought her up as her own. When they died, this girl, now a woman, became one of the richest women in the Philippines. *(What was her name? I can't remember, says my mother. But she was very famous.)* Let's call her Doña Felipa.

Now, this woman never married. She never had children of her own. But she was so grateful for what her adoptive parents had done for her that she decided she would adopt girls from all over the Philippines, so that she could give them the same chances she had. She adopted seventeen girls *(sometimes it's seventeen; sometimes it's nine; sometimes it's twenty and more)*. Seventeen girls who came from all over the islands, of all ages. Your grandmother was one of those girls. *(So Lola was an orphan? No, her parents were still alive. But they let her be adopted because they knew she would have a better life. Your great-grandfather was a carpenter you know, and very artistic – he could carve any picture into wood.)* Lola was never one of the favourites though, because she was already eight years old when Doña Felipa found her *(sometimes she was eight; sometimes twelve; sometimes older)* and her favourites were, inevitably, those girls who had been adopted when they were babies and knew no other mother than she. The girls used to all live together in a big house, and the adventures they had!

Once, when Doña Felipa was away, some of the girls decided they wanted to go out and have some ice-cream. So they plotted to steal some money out of Doña Felipa's petty cash. Your Lola said no, of course. She told them that it would be wrong to take the money. But she was overruled and what could she do but go with them? They decided to only take one note. They didn't know how much it was worth because they didn't understand about money. So the girls all went into the city and went to the ice-cream parlour. They handed the owner the note and told him to give them ice-cream until the money ran out. But Doña Felipa was so rich that a single note of her money would buy more ice-cream than nine *(or seventeen; or twenty and more)* girls could ever eat. Each time they finished their dessert, the owner would bring them another, saying, 'the money has not run out yet'. And it never ran out, because before that could happen all the girls were sick, and went home, and were sick some more.

(So is Lola rich too? No. Let me tell you what happened.) Doña Felipa, with all the money in the world, could not read or write. *(Why? I don't know why.)* Perhaps the old Spanish couple believed that with all the wealth she would inherit, Doña Felipa would have no need of an education. Perhaps they would not have educated a girl anyway, even if she was Spanish. We'll never know. Whatever the reason, Doña Felipa, richest woman in the Philippines, was illiterate. All her financial affairs were looked after by lawyers, and accountants *(that is, men)*. Every so often she would be asked to sign something *(how could she sign if she couldn't write?)*, which she did, trusting the men. And she would sign, and she would sign, until one day she was told she had no money left. *(How could that be? When a single note can buy more ice-cream than twenty and more girls can consume in an afternoon, how could the money run out?)*

By this time, all the girls had grown up and moved away. Doña Felipa went to Mary, one of the girls she had adopted as a baby, her favourite.

She went to Mary and told her what the lawyers had said. Mary looked at the papers.

'Why did you sign these?' she asked.

'I was told I had to. I didn't know what they said.'

And Mary shook her head.

Doña Felipa, richest woman in the Philippines, died penniless. And the worst of it was, few of the girls she had adopted would help her. All those babies she had loved. Except for Lola of course. That was Doña Felipa's greatest regret, that she hadn't loved your grandmother more.

'If only I'd known, Femi, that you would be the one I could trust.' *(Who's Femi? That's your Lola of course. That's her name. Eufemia. Femi.)*

Isn't it sad? Isn't it beautiful? It's a true story. *(My mother would always end the story this way: this is a true story.)*

But at other times, the story of my grandmother was simply this: 'Lola? Oh, she's Pampamga. They come from the mountains. It means she's a good cook.' If this is true, the gift was not passed on. My dad, fed up of the smell of burnt rice, did all the cooking; and now my boyfriend, after the first few meals I served up early in our relationship, does all the cooking in our home.

My mother never read to my brother and me, but she told us a bedtime story every night. Family histories of sisters who came back from the dead without their souls, or grieving mothers who went mad after the death of children and who ran after soldiers to try and kill them like dogs. Sometimes she would tell us fairytales that everyone knew, like Snow White and Sleeping Beauty and Cinderella. But most of all she liked to tell us stories of vampires, or werewolves; or tales of children who happened to have the same names as my brother and me, and who were eaten by aliens because they talked to strangers. Sometimes she would pretend that she wasn't really our mother, that inside her body she was really Count Dracula or Frankenstein or the Wolfman, and I would scream and scream and scream, and my brother, younger than me by seventeen months, would cry.

My mother had three books, all in hardback: a DIY book; a thick, small-print history book with red cloth covers called *The Japanese Imperial Conspiracy*; and *The AA Book of British Towns*. She claimed that once she also had a Bible, and the *Complete Works of William Shakespeare*, but that they were lost after I was born. When I left school and went to work in a clothes shop, I spent the first money I earned on books and hid them in my wardrobe. Now I have started to send my mother books with my name inside. She reads the stories and says, 'but nobody talks like that.'

I can only tell stories that are written down. If I open my mouth to speak, the words die on my tongue, or they come out in the wrong place, in the wrong story.

Boston Diptych

Benjamin Mellor

I: Dolls, 1954

The eyes are wide. They cannot address
the helplessness which has lingered in
the airless peace of each glass case:
to have survived. To have been stronger than

a moment. To be the hostages ignorance
takes from time and ornament from destiny. Both.
To be the present of the past. To infer the difference
with a terrible stare. But not feel it. And not know it.

Eavan Boland, 'The Dolls Museum in Dublin'

'Say, what happened to this one?' John Bloomfield fingered the glass of the walnut display cabinet like a child in an aquarium as Nancy Geraghty entered carrying a tray of steaming cups.

'You'll have to have tea, I've no coffee.' She set down the tray and crossed to where he stood, pulling a tissue from her sleeve and briskly wiping away the greasy print his pudgy digit had left on the pane. John went to the couch and sat down. She stared for a moment at the space on the shelf he'd pointed to; a gold beribboned presentation box, long since vacated, positioned amongst her abundant collection of dolls.

She'd called her Milly. Precocious pouting cheeks and blonde hair done up in a pretty lace dress; Daddy had bought her on a business trip to Paris when Nancy was six. A conduit for years of unexpressed affection. He was busy, always. Big man in textiles. Layman at the local parish church in Dolphin's Barn, Glasnevin. Our Lady of Dolours. But there were secrets too, silent tension erupting into muffled rows behind slammed doors. And then the fighting broke out. Nancy and her sisters never knew of their father's involvement until the constabulary came for him that morning. 29th April, 1916. He was released a year later – a year of hissed threats and hateful spittle in the streets – and soon secured passages for the girls to sail to America. *For your own safety*. An echo of a foghorn blast and the acrid odour of black steam recalled the long voyage from Dublin to Boston. The nauseating claustrophobia of the cabin; her envy as her two sisters slept. Loco Parentis. *You're a young woman now*. Up on deck, angry tears, silenced by the din of turbines, splashed on a surprised ceramic face. *You're a young woman now. Put away childish things.* She'd held Milly over the rail by her pale arms and in an instant of rage followed by a flood of regret, released her grip; lunging after her in vain as she fell into the churning white waters.

'She was lost. Moving.'

Nancy walked slowly to her armchair and picked up a cup of tea to warm herself.

'Now what do you have to say to me Mr Bloomfield? I have things to do.'

'John, please. And I do appreciate you giving up your time like this Ma'am.'

He flashed her one of his winning smiles. It went unreturned.

'Well, as you know, I'm from the Federal Highway Administration, working on this new expressway system. We realise there's been some... opposition, to the final phase of the project and as you're so... prominent in that opposition, we thought it would be a good idea to come talk to you, try to iron out a few creases. So to speak.'

Nancy sipped her tea in silence.

'You see, with the central artery nearing completion it's really essential that work gets under way on the inner belt or the system just won't work. You see without it, the volume of traffic that we predict on the central highway over the next ten years will leave it unable to cope, choked.'

'I see. And how many people do your predictions tell you will be displaced Mr Bloomfield? Another twenty thousand? Another thousand buildings demolished or would you be hoping to break that record this time?'

'Naturally we aim to keep disruption to a minimum, Mrs Geraghty. But let me assure you, this is a creative project, not a destructive one. Sure, you gotta crack eggs to make an omelette, but at least half the buildings we plan to take down are substandard structures. They'd be removed by urban renewal in the next few years anyway. This highway will boost development, eat out the abscess of our slums and create new opportunities for the people of Boston that far outweigh the inconveniences.'

Nancy met his words with a cold stare. The slick, high-minded patter had an unsettlingly familiar ring. The rhetoric of progress. The good of the people. Echoes of the politicians' war-talk her husband Tom had imitated when he vowed to join the fighting in 1941. Duty, patriotism. The war to end wars (part two). But just over five years since she'd lost him, the boys had been sent off to Korea on their next crusade. When would it stop? Were they already planning the next war, the next road?

Bloomfield attempted another smile but it withered when it met her frosty glare. He reached for his briefcase, snapping it open on the antique coffee table.

'So...that's the community benefit anyway, let me show you an example of the, the personal gain, you could stand to make here.'

He pulled out two photographs. The first was of the house in which they were sitting. Her house. It was a clapboard bungalow, a little shabby but care-worn, with a small neat lawn. The second was much grander, brand new with two floors, an attic and a sweeping veranda. Nancy noticed that while hers was photographed front-on, making it seem smaller than it actually was, the second house was shot from an angle which displayed the perspective of its dramatic lines to full effect.

'This is an example of the kind of mark-up in property that relocated residents can expect. As you can see, the improvement is considerable.'

It was strange seeing an image of her home like that; an object in miniature. She'd lived there so long it had become like an extension of herself, a place where she and her memories dwelt silently together. Tom's job had moved them around a lot but they'd eventually settled back in Boston for nearly ten years before he joined the army. And it was now nearly another ten since she'd lost him.

'Mr Bloomfield, I live alone. What would I be wanting with a big house like that?'

He shifted uncomfortably in his seat.

'Well…Family?'

'Both my sisters are married, their children grown up. One lives in Ohio, the other in Florida. There's room here should they want to stay but mostly I visit them. I have no children of my own.'

There was a long, sticky silence.

'Mrs Geraghty, I must stress the importance of this project, not only to the local community but to the nation as a whole…'

'You *have* stressed it Mr Bloomfield. You have stressed it in your numerous letters and you have stressed it here today. And *I* have made it clear I will not be moved.'

She rose and walked calmly to the window, looking out to the road beyond.

'When I was a child, the city I grew up in, Dublin, was a great city of walkers. People thought nothing of walking four or five miles to play a game of cards or have a drink with a friend. There was still a sense of community then, the place still had a heart. As I got older more and more cars replaced the horses and carts. And unrest was brewing in the streets. My father sent us here after the Rising. For safety. Though with the rationing, the strikes and the fighting, we could hardly tell the difference. I've seen a lot of this country over the years, I've seen the way it's changed, the way we're always told that growth must increase exponentially. But there are those of us who prefer life at a more pedestrian pace, on a closer scale, the view from the porch. I've been moved about my whole life, Mr Bloomfield, by men and their roads, their wars. I didn't choose to lead this opposition, people just chose to follow me. So if there's nothing else, I'm afraid I must get on with my day.'

John Bloomfield looked at his feet like an admonished schoolboy. Finding nothing to say, he stood, replacing his hat on his head.

'Thanks for the tea,' he said, and shuffled out.

Nancy walked over to the display cabinet in the corner and looked at her collection, each one similar, but different in some small detail, to the one who'd once sat in the empty box.

II: Buoys, 2004

The Aquarium is gone. Everywhere,
giant finned cars nose forward like fish;
a savage servility
slides by on grease.

Robert Lowell, 'For the Union Dead'

Jim lingered on the last stanza of Robert Lowell's 'For the Union Dead', which he'd cut from the *Boston Globe* when it was printed in 1959. He'd had it framed, and when he opened the boatyard six years later he hung it above his new desk in the small but proud office. It was a golden year.

Faded and yellow now, though still legible, the poem hung next to a black and white photograph taken the day the yard opened. A picture of Tess, beaming, with the newly-arrived Jennifer-Rose in her arms; the glossy sign, now peeling, proclaiming *James Hook – Boat Repairs.* Golden.

'Oh Jim, it's so maudlin,' she'd said. 'And since when were you the sort of guy that reads poetry?'

He'd wanted to explain how the sentiments had affected him, the way the rhythm made the lines slide and bump together like boat hulls in the harbour. Lines about roughshod progress; personal memories and public memorials; wars remembered, and bitterly forgotten.

'Guess it just spoke to me,' he shrugged. And left it at that.

Jim put the frames carefully in the cardboard box with the last of his things; thirty-eight years of sunlight leaving their permanent shadow on the wall. He'd been packing all morning and now, despite the boxes jostling for space amidst the sparse office furniture, the place felt unfamiliarly large; a feeling underscored by the echo of every footfall across the creaking floorboards. Only the smell was reassuring: dusty pine, salt air and engine oil from the soaked-in black patterns on the floor when bad weather had turned the office into a workshop.

Jim stopped to take a sip of sweet black coffee. Just the desk left. It was made of heavy beech, a roll-top like a story-book treasure chest and four large drawers. He opened the top one, filled with pens and tools, minor engine parts and grease-stained manuals. At the back sat a child's shoebox filled with cotton wool, inside of which a small, white-faced doll with blonde hair pouted her china cheeks in a lace-work dress stained by the sea. Jim took her out and smiled at her permanent expression of wide-eyed surprise, as if it had frozen on her face the moment she fell in the water. He'd found her floating in the marina one day, a couple of years after Tess had died and Jenny returned to California to finish her studies. He was puttering in from a particularly unfruitful morning's fishing under the insistent pace of the little blue-fin's two-stroke engine when he saw her bobbing there amongst the buoys like a piece of fragile driftwood. The delicate stitching on her dress and her finely finished face suggested she might be valuable, so he'd dried her carefully and kept her safe. He'd decided to save the doll for the day Jenny settled down and made him a grandfather, quietly hoping for a girl. But he'd near as given up on that now.

'Ahoy, Captain!'

Jim jumped, dropping the doll on the desk. He was angry at first but quickly calmed when he saw the familiar face.

'Scott! You trying to give an old man heart attack? Why you here anyway, no school today?'

'Sorry, I didn't mean to scare you. It's lunchtime, thought I'd come see if you needed some help.'

Jim had hired Scott a few years previously when he finally admitted to himself he could do with some assistance around the place. Scott had come to him, an eager boy with a keen interest in all things marine, asking if he could do some odd jobs around the yard in return for learning about boats and engines and the sea. Despite a certain reluctance to disturb his solitude, which had become as familiar to him as family, Jim acquiesced. His fingers were getting arthritic, and his left hip was telling the strain of compensating for the artificial half of his right leg. And besides, Scott's contagious enthusiasm was hard to turn away.

Scott called him Captain on account of his surname and his missing limb, not that you could see it to look at, only when he walked. Jim had suffered this tedious moniker ever since he returned home; people always thought they were the first to come up with it.

It had incensed him to begin with, like a false honour bestowed on him, a tongue-in-cheek commemoration from a nation eager to forget. There'd been no 1945 ticker tape and confetti for his homecoming; even the spit and derision that met the boys returning from Vietnam twenty years later would have been better than quiet indifference and a condescending nickname. But there was a sort of playful respect in the way Scott said it that was disarming. Too young to mean any harm.

'Petty Officer Third Class actually,' he'd corrected once. 'But I guess it don't trip off the tongue so good.'

'Is that where you…?'

'Yup.' Jim saved him the embarrassment. 'Wonsan, North Korea. I was an engineer on the *USS Dextrous*. Minesweeper. Had a fault with one of the pistons one day so I went up on deck looking for the chief engineer. Coulda waited but I was young, keen. Like you. Anyway, got hit by a shore battery, wrong place, wrong time. Next thing I know I wake up on the hospital ship, Consolation. With this…' His gaze dropped to his leg. There was silence.

'You ever thought of joining the forces, Scott?'

'Well, I…'

'Well don't.'

When the letter arrived Jim hadn't known how to break it to the boy. He'd known it was coming but it had taken so long he'd almost convinced himself it wasn't. The land had been earmarked for compulsory clearance when the Big Dig project was first being planned in the eighties. But re-routing Boston's traffic over and under the city in order to remove the public eyesore of the John Fitzgerald Expressway was a long and gradual process, like a tumour growing beneath the surface. If you didn't visit the parts of the city where the bridges and tunnels were being built, which Jim didn't, and you kept up your own quiet routine, which Jim did, it was relatively easy to forget that it was happening at all. Until the letter came.

'Well, thanks for dropping by but as you can see, I'm near as done. Van's coming to pick it all up this afternoon…You could join me for some pie at the Rosebud though?'

They stepped outside and made their way slowly down the crumbling timber steps into the yard. Across the harbour the *USS Constitution*, the oldest navy warship still in commission, was being prepared for its monthly ritual sail into the bay to fire a solitary cannon shot. Its billowing sails, supported by masts like pylons, puffed asthmatically in the wind. All along the chain-link fence hung buoys, collected by Jim over the years, like faded baubles on a tree that's lost its needles. Against the gleaming white shapes undulating in the marina, bouncing pearls of sunlight off their chrome trimmings, the shabby buoys looked out of place. But for Jim they were important. Each one told a different story, each had been a marker for someone, a place to moor their craft and bring it home.

'*Relinquunt Omnia Servare Rem Publicam*. Know what that means, Scott?'

'Well I seen it on that poem you had on the wall but I never knew what it meant.'

'*They gave all for the public good*,' he said, then quietly again to himself, '*They gave all for the public good*.'

He turned to Scott and the spark of a smile flickered over his lips, dying as he looked around the yard once more.

In the diner, Jim sipped his coffee slowly while Scott tapped his spoon against the mouth of the sugar pourer.

'I dunno, it just seems so unfair. Couldn't you protest, stop them building it?'

'If there's one thing I've learnt Scott, it's that you can't stop progress. If it didn't get done now, it'd only be something else further down the line. There was opposition back when the expressway was first built, just after I came home from the war. People protested against being moved, knocking down houses. And that's partly why they say they need to do what they're doing now, the system never worked properly. One generation just handed it on to the next.'

'So what you gonna do?'

'I have the money they paid me. Got a place near Cape Cod, where I grew up. Take a boat, do some fishing. I'm kinda looking forward to it really.'

'Can I...maybe come fishing with you one time?'

Jim smiled. 'Sure you can, Scott. I'd like that.'

As they said goodbye back at the yard there was an awkward moment where neither knew whether a handshake or a hug was more appropriate. In the end it was a clumsy combination of both, but the grip was tightly held. Few words were spoken; neither of them wanting to admit the tightness swelling in their throats.

Jim felt the occasion called for some sort of gesture, and he'd considered giving Scott the doll, but decided against it in case he thought it a little fruity. And besides, there was something else that made him want to keep her. She'd come to mean more to him than just a child's toy found floating, waiting to be passed on. Wherever she'd come from she'd probably been moved about enough. Some things you had to hold on to.

East of No East

Editor: Daithidh MacEochaidh

When is East, East?

Daithidh MacEochaidh

The East is the start of the exotic, from the Far East, to India to the Middle East or Eastern Europe. We neither understand the term exotic nor the term East, we smother vast, diverse, complexities under a blanket term and understand nothing. We no longer understand ourselves, having forgotten how much we owe the East, whether that be in the realm of mathematics, medicine, music or religion. We have forgotten that the biggest myth-making mechanism that we have is an Eastern religion, that Christianity was founded in the East, that we owe a debt of soul to the Eastern Greeks, Armenians, Coptic Egyptians and Ethiopians who were the first Christians after the strictly Messianic Jews. We have forgotten our debt to the Eastern Exotic in a thousand ikons of white Christs, made over in blond and blue eyes and the long, straight Northern European nose that looks down upon us. We forget that the wise men came from further East, India, as did our very languages and pre-Christian myths; we forget our ties to the East in a thousand pogroms against Jews, reconquistas against Muslims, blind prejudice against the Roma.

Words, back to words, we don't know how to describe the East, the exotic. We are told that Europe, the new Europe, has taken a shift East. But these are empty words. The money is still in Frankfurt, Paris and London. The phrase is emptied of meaning by its endemic imprecision, is Latvia east? Bulgaria is east, but is Gdansk east? Europe forgets notions of geography lumping the unknown as the East and thus ironing out all differences, all cultures, creating an unknowable symbol that references nothing or anything. We have a word, it fails to denote anything other than prejudices, misconceptions and vague wave of the hand notions of infantile geography.

Here, we have a glimpse of the East. We have words, meanings, stories from Eastern Europe. The East declares itself in its own words, albeit translated. Here is the chance to listen, to know and to enjoy fresh, energetic writing from a part of Europe that has been rendered dumb by our crass label. East is not East. East is a term that describes our ignorance. These stories from an Eastern European country, from Bulgaria, from contemporary Bulgarian writers, begin to unwrite the empty token 'exotic' into awareness, understanding and delight.

My heartfelt thanks go to the writers featured in this collection, in particular Zdravka Evtimova who has been such a resource and help in bringing new writing and writers to English-speaking audiences both here and with her work for Skrev Press.

Read on, take the next page East…

The Six-Room Flat
Zdravka Evtimova

I was carefully curling her thin hair that I had dyed from sickly blonde to russet ginger more times than I could remember. I was using ancient silver rollers with the initials of the German company Kipheuer-Witsch, her skull under my fingers as brittle as paper, her shoulders almost intangible under the heavy folds of her brocade dress, that made her old skin twitch as I moved about her. It felt as if her soul was about to abandon her, disgusted with the silver rollers, loathing the brocade that weighed far more than the woman herself.

'My dear,' she often addressed me, but I was neither dear nor hers: I felt the cold silver of Kipheuer-Witsch in her words. Her vowels were even and calm like an autumn day. Days and nights had blended into the smooth paste of her voice that told me about her husband, an eminent factory owner who had graduated in fine arts from the University of Vienna. A brilliant violin player, who had inherited his mother's sugar factories, an intellectual whom fate had tossed away in the insignificant country town, smelling of sweat and boredom, a settlement, which was bearable only in spring because then the squalor was concealed under the blossoms of cherry trees. Her husband would play the violin in the evenings, she would listen to him while their little son would frolic by the fountains in the small park.

No, Mrs Baeva would never allow the onus of the sugar factory to mutilate her heir's life; she despised the aroma of caramelised sugar, a poisonous transparent cloud which engulfed the whole town.

I couldn't care less about Mrs Baeva's husband or her son. She had placed an advertisement in a local newspaper, in which I had wrapped my sandwich by accident: some cheese, tomatoes, plus a baked pepper. The elderly lady wrote in her advertisement she would bequeath her gorgeous six-room apartment in the center of Sofia to the person willing to take care of her till death. There were eleven other women who for such a prize were more than prepared to minister to the old lady till she met her maker. To my amazement, she made us all recite poetry. I had hated poetry all my life – guys often tried to convince me that I had beautiful eyes and after I gave them what they wanted the prevailing number of them declared I was a slut. I wouldn't like to use the other vulgar word that guys called me now and then. You all know it, but I do not resort to obscenities even in my mind. Mrs Baeva could hear my thoughts. Whenever words like 'asshole' or 'faggot' crept into my vocabulary, she fined me 100 lev per rude phrase. I could say farewell to my salary if I enjoyed three dirty expressions a month.

When I uttered an indecent phrase from the Bulgarian vocabulary, Mrs Baeva bristled up and her soul made best efforts to extricate itself from her thin hair and Kipheuer-Witsch rollers. I knew what was at the roots of her troubles: she strongly suspected her son was gay. Actually, she not only suspected; her son Dennis had lived with a young man for seven years now. When Dennis visited his mother, the two of them stood in front of the window, overlooking the park with the broken swings, and wept. I couldn't tell you why they cried their hearts out. The truth was their pretty faces glistened in a profusion of tears. Her son had her exquisite shoulders that twitched exactly like Mrs Baeva's, so I supposed his soul, too, was as sensitive and itchy as hers.

'My dear, he was a treasure,' Ma'am explained to me most of the days while I combed her hair; she meant her husband. 'Je lui adore,' she told me in French and when I stared at her blank-faced, she heaved a deep sigh and translated the damned sentence for me: 'I adore him'. I couldn't care less, of course, but she made a habit of starting the day with 'Je lui adore'. Often she would ask me to open the mahogany chest of drawers: I had never imagined that a puny chest like that could be so expensive. She made me polish it with a special paste that her son brought from Vienna, and the poor mahogany wood shone with the energy of the moon and the sun combined. Your arse would shine like the moon, too, if you polished it with that Vienna paste. My eyes hurt on account of the mahogany, but I polished the chest all the same. So, her husband, the treasure, played the violin every night: nocturne after nocturne, sonata after sonata until Mrs Baeva felt blissfully happy. He kissed her goodnight to which she responded with a grateful smile, half asleep. On the other hand, their son had a nurse, a young Mademoiselle, gentle and refined who recited Schiller in German, Byron in English and Baudelaire in French. The Mademoiselle could play the violin, the cello and the pianoforte. She played different concertos so magnificently that Mrs Baeva's son and husband wept silent tears by her side. Once in a blue moon, Mr Baeva – when he was not utterly exhausted by the problems of the sugar factory – played the violin with the nurse and these were miraculous evenings, no doubt. What a pity that the lad asked his mother to hire a man to be his governess. Indeed, Dennis had no appetite at all, he pined and lost weight, he was such a delicate curly boy who recited Baudelaire in French and Schiller in German, but whenever Mademoiselle approached him and stretched across the table to touch his hand, the kid felt dizzy. If she remained in his room late in the night to read to him, then in the morning Dennis woke up covered in a horrible rash that mutilated his marble-white skin…

Before Mrs Baeva reached the point where her son's marble skin was totally marked, I had usually managed to curl one third of her hair although it was as thin as laser rays. I knew what would come next: she wept harassed by the memory of miserable Dennis and his ruined complexion. I gave her mineral water; she touched my hand, her skin always cold, icy: perhaps death was already in her fingers and the chill came from the world beyond. It did not bother me, I was accustomed to touching death and obeying her usual order, 'Go and clean my son's house, Monika.'

I promptly promised I'd clean her son's and his boyfriend's house, meanwhile thinking how I was to smuggle Miladin, a boy I slept with from time to time, into Mrs Baeva's six-room flat. The walls of the flat were guarded against robberies: a thick network of black wires encompassed them. Ma'am had a safety system installed, which signalled the intrusion of gangsters, thieves, rapists, spiders, rodents and cockroaches by producing sounds of a differentiated pitch. Miladin always visited me wearing one of my dresses so I told Mrs Baeva he was our new charwoman. The charwoman was allowed to enter the flat twice a week. She cleaned its spacious six rooms furnished with Vienna divans, cabinets and tables from the eighteenth century. Mrs Baeva was as good as blind without her glasses, so she asked to touch and check the charwoman's cheek – smooth skin was her obsession.

Maybe I had forgotten to mention that when Ma'am chose me among the eleven other competitors for the job, the first thing she did was to touch my cheeks. She rejected professional nurses on the grounds they could not recite, they inadvertently blurted out impolite remarks or she thought their voices sounded ugly. I suspected the major reason she flunked them was that the skin of their faces did not feel smooth. She touched all cheeks in turn and selected me, because my skin was as smooth as a polished shoe. Quite apart from that I had succeeded in stammering out a whole stanza of Vazov's poem 'I am a Bulgarian'. Alas, that was a flash in the pan, for later she made me recite Schiller and Shakespeare and I could not utter an articulate sound. I kept mum as if I was a dead fish. Yet I was the only one among the eleven competitors who knew these guys were poets although I hated poetry. Mrs Baeva said, 'You are my girl,' and I was.

Ma'am touched Miladin's cheek as well. He had fine bone structure and enormous blue eyes. I made him shave painstakingly before pouring French belle's perfume all over him – Mrs Baeva adored French scents and unlike her eyes which couldn't tell a cow from her servant, her nose could distinguish between all of the twelve different perfumes I spilt over Miladin. Sometimes she and Miladin wept together. She had somehow managed to move him with the story about the man she loved; that fortunate individual, of course, was not her husband, who in spite of all his accomplishments and indisputable qualities was 'simply a good friend'. The guy she was in love with was perfect. She had never used the word 'lover' when she described him although he undoubtedly was an able one. Oh, what a shameful blemish that would be for his blessed heart and gentle soul. She adored him.

This blessed individual joined his maker on account of excessive consumption of alcohol or maybe because he was one of the few drug addicts of his time. Whatever the truth, I often saw Miladin and Mrs Baeva weep in unison for her beloved. Miladin sobbed most sincerely and Ma'am was sure he put his heart in his tears, although as I said before her eyes were as good as if they had been gouged out. She had an eerie sixth sense of fakers and caught you on the spot if you but tried to trick her. I had made it a rule with Ma'am: better keep mum like a fried trout and let her touch your cheek than feign sincerity. I let her fingers on my cheek reminisce about her own beauty in her youth. She used to be a fascinating young minx, she said, and 'my complexion was like yours at present, Monika'. Somehow I couldn't make out the knot of silver rollers in her voice, which was accustomed to purchasing and selling, neither could I make out the tears in her thinning eyes.

I could play no musical instrument; I loathed violins, sonatas and nocturnes, but 'God has blessed you with an angelic voice, my dear,' Mrs Baeva said and asked me to sing to her. I knew most of the hits of Metallica but she shook uncontrollably whenever I attempted to sing them to her. She coerced me into cramming an Italian song and although I couldn't make head nor tail of what it said I sang it to her, softly, so softly you could hear the clock knit the minutes into a rope around your neck. I crooned and cooed the Italian words until she began to weep, half of her hair captured in the rollers, the other half hanging like gossamer down her skull.

Miladin sat immobile on the piano stool in the antechamber. I often wondered how it was possible for his backside not to contract paralysis. But when I tucked Mrs Baeva in and turned to look at him, I saw that his face was sopping wet – he did get upset about the song – Ma'am had translated it into Bulgarian for him. The song, of course, told a story about unrequited love. Miladin was so moved upon hearing it that he could not make love for a while. To be honest with you, a situation like that was highly frustrating for me. I hadn't given him my best dress to have him by my side soft like dough, teardrops all over him, while Mrs Baeva snored in her mahogany bed.

I imagined what would happen if she discovered Miladin was not a woman. She might kick me out or might give Miladin the boot and keep me. Actually, I had chosen him on account of his ability to squeeze into my dress and look like a girl in it. I liked the blue look in his eyes, though.

One evening Baeva's son met Miladin who had dolled himself up in my dress. I expected some sort of disaster but Dennis remarked casually, 'That is our new servant girl, is it not?' and gave Miladin his old shirt as a present. I should have smelled a rat back then.

As I curled the second half of Mrs Baeva's hair, she would often tell me that, perhaps, it had been her fault that her son had developed the way he had. She knew very well that Dennis's skin blistered on account of his nurse's presence, so one night when the lad pleaded with his mother, his eyes brimming with tears, to hire a boy to take care of him, she had given in. She had hoped that Dennis would get accustomed to men's company, learn to play men's games and behave like a man. Yet, it had the opposite effect…What a pity, Mrs Baeva's husband said grieving over the beautiful night concerts with Mademoiselle. They could not recite together Schiller, Goethe and Heine any more. He could only bury his head in the heaps of sugar that his factory produced, and lament his days in the world of gruff workers and accountants who would bamboozle him into going bankrupt in a flash. Mademoiselle was so sorry too…an inordinately sensitive girl that no factory owner of repute would hire. Who else would want a love-sick nurse sprawling on the sitting room floor in your villa!

So the family hired a lad to take care of Mrs Baeva's son. He was an exceptionally civilised young guy who recited William Blake and Hoelderlin, but, alas, his family went bust in the cruel crisis of 1940. That lad won everybody with his refinement, erudition and elegance and what a pity again! Several months after they hired him, Mrs Baeva happened to search for her son's silk shirt in the wardrobe in his room. The thing she saw left her broken-hearted: her son, already a young man himself, and his male nurse were naked together, God forgive me the obscene phrase I resorted to! For a fleeting instant Ma'am didn't know how she should react: if she announced her presence she could inflict a spiritual trauma on her son that wouldn't heal. She chose to circumspectly withdraw and on the very next day she asked her husband to fire the male nurse.

Mrs Baeva's son fell into a black depression, then was hit by a crisis, a disease-like state during which he came up in an itchy rash. His marble skin looked as if it had been covered with popcorn. He'd be okay, Mrs Baeva told herself and made a firm decision – an act I could relate to the knot of clanging Kipheuer-Witsch silver rollers in her voice.

Another event, a more tragic one occurred soon after that: her boy Dennis sold his books – by Goethe, Schiller, Heine and all the rest of them, he pawned the presents he had received for his birthdays: a gold ring, a diamond, his horse La Rochefoucault, and even hawked several pairs of his shoes. Then Dennis rushed to seek for his male nurse. This romantic hunt had been in vain – Mrs Baeva had prudently sent the individual to Pirot, a town in Macedonia, to an asylum for aristocratic young men with psychotic disorders. At that point of the tale, the silver rollers curled Mrs Baeva's voice into a wire that could strangle anyone. In the long run, the male nurse ran away from the asylum and embarked on a dangerous trip back to Bulgaria, begging for food and small change all the way down to Sofia, to his beloved Dennis, Mrs Baeva's son.

Miladin had already heard that tale twice. The first time he listened to it his face was soaked with tears like a freshly irrigated lawn. Mrs Baeva personally checked his cheeks and was deeply gratified by the charwoman's sympathy and good heart. Miladin was really upset; he remained soft almost half of the night, but as I had already pointed out, that could hardly be tolerated by me.

I convinced Mrs Baeva we needed another charwoman, a more energetic one, and I substituted Miladin for another guy, a burlier one. He had a wiry beard no matter how diligently he shaved, and when Mrs Baeva touched his cheek she felt sorely disappointed. She declared that people who had suffered from small pox made her think of old age, varicose veins and wrinkles. Thus Miladin came back, meeker than ever, and tried to convince me he had learnt his lesson well.

Whenever he wept, he dried his tears with a towel and made best efforts to conceal them from me. Alas, one day he recited 'Freude, schoene Goetterfunken' by Schiller while staring at a photograph in a silver frame, which showed Mrs Baeva as a young woman of the beau monde. The old photo made it clear that Ma'am had just given birth to a most beautiful son smiling happily in his mother's arms. Actually, Miladin recited only the first stanza of 'Freude'. He reiterated that absurd stanza muttering the German words like prayer every time he passed by Mrs Baeva's photograph. She must have turned heads when she was young. It was the most logical thing that a beau should appear; at this point I again eschewed the popular word 'lover'.

Every Tuesday and Thursday Miladin placed a red rose in front of Mrs Baeva's photograph. Occasionally he addressed me as 'Natalia' – that was her personal name. In the beginning it really annoyed me but when I saw that 'Natalia' honed his skills, I let him call me the way he pleased. That didn't last long. On Thursday, before Miladin got his salary from Ma'am, he most unexpectedly declared, 'Ma'am, I am not a woman. I am a man. I admire your son. *Je lui adore*!'

That sentence rendered us both speechless, awestruck.

No more do I curl Ma'am's hair using the ancient silver rollers with the initials of the German company Kipheuer-Witsch. That day she had them all buried in a big flowerpot. We purchased some soil from a park in Vienna for that flowerpot and her rollers. Now and then, she weeps tears of grief, letting them drop into the flowerpot, into the very heart of Kipheuer-Witsch.

The Island of the Blessed

Boyan Biolchev

The old women were crawling across the yellowing common towards the cemetery, clutching glowing flowers, grown by the troughs of the dying water fountains in the little yards of the village. From the sea, a sharp north-easterly wind was blowing and the old women staggered in its gushes. The dead man lay in the coffin fixing his closed eyes on the azure sky. By his side, there was the hand-wagon on which he had been brought.

Some conversation came floating from the grave.

The two men had abandoned the shovels and had hidden from the wind in the pit. The summer fishermen's hangover clung to their faces. One of them was rather thin, with a head like a pin. The head of the other man was stuck between the shoulders without a neck.

'The wire in this shipment is strong,' he said. 'At home, I have some left over from last year. On it, Gosho couldn't have hung himself at all. It would have broken.'

'He didn't want to hang himself last year,' the thin man replied, 'I've been talking with him.'

'And why did he want to this year?'

The thin man gazed at him and shrugged his shoulders. After a short pause, one after the other the two men drank in huge swills from the bottle and left it in the wet corner of the pit because it was July, despite the wind.

Right then, the head of one of the old women showed from above. The thin man waved her away in anger.

'We aren't through, yet. Can't you see?'

Apparently, the old woman saw that. She saw the bottle too. It was clear that the wailing cries had been postponed indefinitely. The old women scuttled submissively and sat down in the shadow of the oaks. The cemetery was like an island in the yellow sea of the woods. Those who had lived here before had uprooted the trees to make room for fields. Only the dead ones had saved a piece of the ancient forest.

'Are we going to dig?' the neckless man asked.

'Gosho is not in a hurry. Why should we be?'

'All right. The priest isn't here, either.'

The thin one gave him a curt look.

'What priest!'

'The village one.'

'You should have brought a priest from the town! Don't you really know anything?'

'What should I know?'

'You're Gosho's cousin, aren't you?'

'I am. That's why I came here to dig the grave.'

'His grave. And do you know why he is going to lie in it? You would see Gosho only during the time of the belted bonito. You all just hang around in that town…'

'I live there.'

The thin man drank from the bottle and with a didactic grimace passed it to the confused cousin. Drinking in a grave conforms to the same rules as any other place. The rakia scorched the throat of the neckless man, too. He smacked his lips and asked, 'What happened? Whoever I ask, they mumble nonsense from which one can't understand anything.'

'Love!' the thin one said knowingly. 'In the winter, a man came and said that he was a priest. He claimed the Synod had sent him to the village. He had a real beard but cursed ever so often and, in the pub, yelled at everybody that we were too dumb. There wasn't a church but there was a priest. Still and all, nobody paid any attention because all our things were like that. His wife was good looking; one would never think that she was a priest's wife. And Gosho lost his head. She twisted him around her little finger; all his money was gone in no time. Right then, they started repairing the dam and the village filled with lorry drivers. Not one did she miss. She robbed them all. Gosho decided to save her and went to the priest. He wanted to complain that the woman had cheated. But the priest said that he wanted to finish his drink first and Gosho should come back and see him some other day. And on the following day, the two of them slipped away because he was not a priest and the whore was not his wife. And Gosho, being a bachelor of fifty, instead of just cursing and forgetting, kept quiet for two months and then kicked the bucket. It seems that some people don't want to live when everything turns out to be what it isn't.'

The thin one was silent for a moment, then he smiled, 'Love. Do you know what love is?'

'What is it?'

'How should I know. I'm an old bachelor, too. Can a normal person live in a god-forsaken village full of old women; forsaken, in addition, by the devil? You can't even find anyone to dig your grave…'

The conversation stalled. The wind was howling in the coffin like a hysterical mourner. The dead man was not really in a hurry. In the shadow, the old women were waiting wearily.

In the grave, life was continuing with the consecutive swills of liquor.

The neckless man was the only one who was frowning because apparently the rakia was not good.

Translated by Todor Shopov

Cherry Orchards

Svetlana Dicheva

The boy looked like a bundle forgotten in the corner. Only the legs that were sticking out showed that it was a huddled body. In the last few days the boy had occupied this spot, looking upon it as his home. He slept practically all the time, night and day, undisturbed by the glaring light or the passing people. In a state of half sleep, his consciousness was unable to perceive the transition from the world of his imagination and the world of dreams. In his short life he had had very little contact with nature but his imagination was nourished from the common cauldron of human experience into which, like small streams, flows everything we have lived through. Trees in blossom like brides draped in veils and laces lured him and gave him the feeling of eternal spring. Although he was only ten years old Ahmed had discovered the important truth that imagination is richer than reality. It was not the astronomic spring that was important, but the spring inside you. He had passed hundreds of times by the cherry tree in blossom in the garden of his grandmother's house, he had brushed aside the branches that had gone wild, without feeling anything inside. Now, when the real cherry tree had long been cut off, cherry orchards bloomed in his mind's eye. A rough kick in his stomach brought him out of his pleasant vision.

'And who are you, bastard?' The face above the leather boots, jeans, and leather jacket was vicious.

Ahmed stirred. He was afraid that the big fellow would beat him to a pulp. Nothing good could come from those half-closed eyes. He got up and nervously beat the dust off his clothes. He didn't want to give the impression of being arrogantly impudent and he said hurriedly, 'My name is Ahmed. I have no home. I thought I could rest here for a while.'

'Didn't it occur to you when you settled down here that you have to pay rent?'

'Well...there was no one here. I didn't know...'

'Now you know. The rent is one thousand levs a day. As you see it's not much. But if you start a business here it will have to go up. Is that clear?' the man said and kicked him again. He wanted to instill fear in the boy. Everybody from the underground society of the underpass feared him and paid him rent. Those who didn't had to sleep under the open sky. This was an underpass, it had its infrastructure and comforts and one had to pay for them.

Ahmed was greatly distressed. Where could he find a thousand levs a day? He had to find a job, no matter how hard it would be. And on top of that he had to eat. Those pressing problems made him forget his beautiful dreams. He sat down on the ground, hugging his knees, and got lost in thought. At one point he heard someone call from the stall opposite him where they sold cheese patties, 'Hey, boy, come over here!'

Behind the opening from which they sold the patties was the wide round face of a woman advanced in years.

'Do they want you to pay?'

'M-hm,' Ahmed nodded.

'And what are you going to do now?'

'I don't know.'

'Come in. The entrance is at the back.'

The oven was at the back too. He could see through its glass door the crispy brown patties. Ahmed nearly choked on his saliva. The fat woman opened the door of the oven, and with a little spatula, took out a piping hot patty and offered it to him.

'Come on, eat it up before you've fainted. Don't try to look heroic. I've been watching you, you haven't eaten anything for days...'

Ahmed broke the patty, not believing his luck. He had forgotten that warming feeling that food gives you. People say that crusty patties melt in your mouth. Nothing of the kind – they disappear.

'What's your name?' The fat lady seemed to be really interested in his name.

'Ahmed.'

'And you're fifteen years old, right?' the woman grinned.

'Fourteen,' he lied.

'Somewhere there,' the woman went on smiling. She was not after all that fat, but she was battered like a pan which a clumsy housewife was always dropping.

'And what's your name?' Ahmed realized that he was really as interested in that woman as he was interested in the blossoming cherry orchards.

'Petranka. You can call me Aunty Peppy.'

Ahmed thought for a while.

'No, I'll call you simply Peppy.'

The woman was slightly embarrassed. She quickly tucked away a white lock under her kerchief. Ahmed stayed with her to help her. He carried the big baking trays, sacks of flour and crates of bottles of cooking oil. He became her right hand. He even started selling patties when she was busy. He was better than her at the accounts. She mended and washed his clothes. She brought him a blanket.

One day she couldn't restrain herself any longer and she told him, 'Ahmed, you smell. When did you last have a bath?'

Ahmed blushed but made up his mind to steal a deodorant from the stall on the corner.

Peppy looked at him as if reading his thoughts. 'You can't hide your stink with toilet water. We'll do something else.'

She brought a bucket and an immersion heater. The bathing campaign was organised in the toilet of the underpass. Against her protests Ahmed insisted bashfully that she should go out…

'But you're just a child, Ahmed. There's nothing to be shy about,' she kept saying in front of the door of the toilet but he kept his teeth firmly clenched.

Later, bathed, refreshed and smelling nice, Ahmed poured out a glass of beer for her. He was very grateful to her.

He decided that her greying hair was attractive and her body looked like risen dough which was suitable material for a crusty patty. The beer and the good looks of her boy made her confide in Ahmed. 'Something good is going to happen to me soon. I know it. I'm certain. My heart tells me that it will,' she said and painted her lips in a haphazard way without looking at herself in a mirror. She was beautiful even without the lipstick but Ahmed discovered that some women lack self-confidence.

And indeed, something did happen but Ahmed did not think it was good at all. The brazen ruffian, the racketeer who ruled over everyone in the underpass, and whose name was Orhan, took Peppy out one evening. She was dolled up like a romantic goose. When she put on a hat he nearly fainted.

'You, nitwit, keep an eye on the area!' Orhan ordered him happily, giving him at the same time a friendly kick. Clearly that man could give expression to his feeling only with his legs.

Peppy returned in the morning. She was very drunk and looked rumpled. She had lost her hat but this did not spoil her good mood. She slept until noon on a makeshift bed of crates. In the meantime Ahmed made and sold cheese patties.

When she opened her eyes she exclaimed, 'Lord, it was so good! I wouldn't have experienced this if I had died earlier. Give me a patty, I'm starving.'

Ahmed gave her the most delicious looking and crusty patty and was surprised to find out that his hand was trembling. In the evening when he huddled in 'his' corner he saw Orhan approach the stall like a fox. He watched the man go in and set upon Peppy's spongy body. She surrendered to his embraces like a thirsty person who had just crossed a desert. Something in Ahmed shrank, he turned his face to the wall and tried to 'see' his blossoming cherry orchards. But he could not see them, every time he saw the trees, he saw amongst the branches, covered with blossoms, Peppy's face, satisfied, disgustingly content. Ahmed tried to chase her away from the blossoming cherries but she stayed as if she was stuck there. A kick broke his vision.

'Scrote, you sleep too early.' Orhan, smiled down at him. Ahmed yearned to smash his face in, but then he was only ten years old. 'Good night, boy, and I want you to know that from now on, you pay nothing, but don't forget how generous your uncle Orhan is!'

Ahmed huddled, retreated to his shell. In the morning he left 'his' corner forever. Petranka looked for him everywhere and asked everyone for news, but in vain. Somewhere, in another corner he was dreaming of his cherries in blossom, desperately trying to chase away a face, which spoiled the vision.

Translated by Vladimir Filipov

Road to Brigitte Bardot

Dimitar Tomov

It was harder at nighttime; the expectation, full of unknowns, without the man who has always been by you. On a night like this, you feel that it is better not to have been born at all, rather than meet the dawn unaware of why everything around you is suddenly different. It had become dark twice since they had brought them here, to this place full of wetness and trees. She could not understand why the only appealing and familiar thing, which reminded her of the world where she used to move, was separated by this cold, woven obstruction, exasperating in its transparency. She tried to jump over it even on the first night. She rose on two legs but her front paws could not reach the edge of the hard metal net in any way. She clawed instinctively at the small rhomboid openings but they would not give in. She did not understand why she did not go along the concrete pathway with the two-legged creatures that moved freely. Until the day before, she walked among them and the man who she remembered from the first moment after birth. This memory merged with the image of her own mother. He had brought her without compunction; the usual curious, well-disposed multitude crowded around but her keeper, habitual as nature – without pulling the bow along the live strings of his cumbersome instrument and extracting from them the magical sounds, which made her bear heart throb and her bulky and clumsy paws dance – that Man who was, for her, unique among men – had abandoned her in this strange place and did not show up for the third day. It was certainly a game because they had brought ten others like her. She knew only Macho. She would see him in the streets of the big city now and then, and the merry, interested crowd would double as soon as they caught sight of two bears in concert. Macho's master had abandoned him too. However Macho did not turn around the fence like her. He lay most of the time. His sides were humping and his fur was torn here and there. She had tried several times to make him move but he just closed his eyes and shook his head despairingly. The others like her turned in circles and made innumerable attempts to realise that they were confined in a certain space: despite the trees, bushes, meadows and formed paths, artificial hills and piled rocks, which resembled cliffs, the area remained fenced. She made sure of that during the two nights she had spent here; yet she would not give in to the new situation even for a moment. There had to be a way out. Her master – where was he, why was he late, why wouldn't he come? Her last recollection of his face did not prefigure any sudden disappearance like this. And his voice did not disclose anything either. 'Come on, Masha,' he had said and the others had been looking smilingly and encouragingly; before knowing it she had found herself in this enclosure; her Rom had mingled with the crowd without even trying to play his music. Some important, costumed people had spoken something, which her bear mind couldn't grasp; since she was young, she had learned how to distinguish the important people and expected, as soon as their talk ended, Mango, her master with the moustache, to cry out, 'Come on, Masha, tread for health.' Some brave fellow from the audience would lie down and she solemnly and proudly would tread on him; the lucky man would get up no less proud and worthy because of his bravado – to have been trodden on by a bear...

These memories seemed distant now but engulfed her – more persistently than the light rain, which had not ceased ever since they had been put behind the lifeless fences. The people from the first day had hidden. Nobody came to let her out. Without realising her instinctive craving for the only life she had known from the moment of her birth – life passing through crowded streets, amidst the noise of automobile horns, shouts and the inevitable dancing before the wide-eyed crowds – without realising her subsequent actions, the vague threat of having been abandoned, that she was alone and had to help herself, filled her with anxiety, which on the third night had turned into worry but not panic. She was trained to refuse to accept and those lessons were mixed with the roaming nature of her stubborn master who took her across the endless world of the overcrowded streets; when attention was not enough or when they chased them away just for of the fact of their presence, they appeared somewhere else where they were wanted and the joy of being the centre of attention never ended.

The night advanced and the wind, which had started suddenly, chased away the clouds. Her wet fur stood on end because of the cold. Some birds began chirping but the birds' disturbance only reminded her of the din which she was missing. In the clear, lightening sky, the moon had risen and the milky way of the large stars enticed with its closeness. She had to start along that way; those were her brethren; she could discern them. She had no way of explaining when she had grasped that her own star contour was marked in the sky. Thousands of times her master and his children, hopping like crickets, had drawn for her, in minimised scale, the enormous constellation with which, even if she did not know that it was called Ursa Major or the Great Bear, she had been taught to believe she had something in common; because to rise before the audience like her celestial brother was part of her show; as soon as she did that number the audience would enthuse with wild cries and her bear heart would sink and her eyes would grow faint not because of the furry coat.

She had risen on her hind legs and her paws did not tremble – outlined by the silver contour of the moonlight. The one in the sky was free shining with the immortality of liberty and, despite the fact that she could not think, she felt that nobody would ever be able to confine behind bars and nets that one up there in the light starry darkness. There had to be a way out.

And she started.

She would stop from time to time, raise her head towards the centrifuge of the stars – her brother danced in her shiny company of glittering celestial eyes – and she would run again with doubled energy. Tonight, her intuition worked faultlessly. Ursa Major pulled her to the north. She reached the fence and made a semi-circle; it was as if she had always known that it would succumb somewhere. She found the opening in the narrow stretch between the corner join. Her coat suffered the most but she could go unharmed out of the incomprehensible territory and could continue in the safe direction.

She could hardly explain why she hurried so much. She ran aware of her intuition to escape from the confined space with only the hope to get back to the one who had left her. In the middle of her bear's run, she did not pay attention to the lightening night: from the east the dawn of the new day flowed in; but the fiery clot kept pulsating in her worn-out soles. She could fall any minute but she would not stop.

She managed to enter the city before the dark had finally left the endless streets, which, from the suburbs, changed into boulevards leading to the heart of this enticing, many-faced, roaring and screaming world.

Light came fast and at the dawn of the coming day they could spot her, crossing the familiar passages. 'Bear! Bear!' They shouted behind her but she did not stop. She had to reach that place with the warm waters, which flowed freely among the enormous buildings. Despite the fact that they soared up everywhere, there was a small spot left, a playground where the audience applauded her most often and where, in addition to the warm aromatic water, she would now and then drink the frothy bitter liquid from brown or green bottles given to her by some grateful bystander.

She reached the statue with the gold head and the bird frozen on her hand. The familiarity of this orienting point pleased her. Right in front, the many-coloured flags were flapping – a motley forest, which she remembered appearing. Most often they would chase her master and her from this place. Here, they would often stop the traffic, not just the two of them, and the shiny cars and the costumed men would become numerous.

She hurried to pass this square. The shouts 'Bear! Catch it!' were increasing and mixed with the car horns, which stopped so that she could go. She saw men in uniforms; they approached in a line but she escaped skilfully the open space, hid behind the columns which supported the familiar buildings. In this corridor, in the middle of the chase and the run, she saw him. In fact, she saw the crickets first. They also saw her first and hopped shouting, 'Daddy, Daddy, Masha!' And they dashed to hug her. At last she stopped. Mango the Rom squatted by a stone column. Their eyes met and he, her master, ran to her; she sat down still. She had found him. Nothing else mattered. People came and came. She and Mango hugged and nobody dared to separate the two of them. In her much-loved creature's hands, the cumbersome string instrument had appeared and the sounds, familiar to her, came out.

'Come on, Masha!'

She did not wait for another invitation.

She got up, fatigue drained out somewhere. Her clumsy legs danced, her furry eyebrows had drawn a curtain over her eyes again and the world was blurring and spreading, flowing out into smudging contours; and she would not stop.

Translation: Todor Shopov

Skin

Editor: Crista Ermiya

Introduction

Crista Ermiya

Skin is a border frontier, the porous barrier between what's on the outside and the inside; appearance and reality. The three stories and two non-fiction pieces collected here are outposts on the frontier, each with a different view across the landscape.

Andrew Clancy's haunting story 'Where It Ends' is both a love story and, literally, the word made flesh. Nicky O'Neill's 'Candle' depicts bodies escaping the confines of their given skin in a story both learned and graphic. Diane Cockburn provides a comic-surreal warning to all country walkers with her story 'Tick-Bite Precautions.'

Katy Massey and Rochita Loenen-Ruiz, with their memoir pieces 'Morphea' and 'My Skin, Us', demonstrate that non-fiction writing is also a creative enterprise, and get under the concept of skin to reveal what is hidden, whether a rare disease, long undiagnosed, or the subtleties of discrimination.

Part I
Flesh

Where It Ends

Andrew Clancy

'cleave'

The word was tattooed across the small of Donna's back. I ran my finger along it, almost surprised that it felt the same as the rest of her skin. A faint perfume rose from her, underneath the smell of cigarettes and whiskey, a hint of lemon and honey.

She stirred in her sleep and I froze, but I needn't have worried; she mumbled something and resumed her easy breathing.

Her back rose and fell evenly in the dim light from the street. Occasionally the sounds of cars moving through the grey dawn broke the silence, and I wondered where they were going, all those darkened drivers.

Every time I saw her tattoo I wanted to ask about it, what it meant, but somehow always forgot. The lettering looked formal, official, Times New Roman or something like that.

I spread my fingers and ran my hand up her back and onto her neck. Her skin was smooth and warm; it glowed in the dim light like a polished thing, metal or stone. I pushed my fingers on, into her hair. It felt good, feeling the black strands gathering in the spaces between my fingers. I turned my hand, gathered a fistful of hair. For a brief moment I thought about pulling it as hard as I could.

But I got up and walked back to my room. I knew I wouldn't sleep for a while.

In the hall the toilet flushed, then started to refill noisily. Outside I could hear footsteps padding softly to my door. 'You awake, Suzie?'

I tried to make my voice sound drowsy, as if I had just been woken.

'Sure, come on in Donna.'

She opened my door, stood silhouetted there, hand on hip. When she spoke there was a tremolo in her voice, a faint vibration.

'What were you doing in my room?' she said.

'I don't know what you mean.'

'Don't play dumb Suzie, I know you were there. I woke up when you were leaving.' She was swaying slightly. Perhaps she was still drunk.

'Christ Donna, it's not so long since you were begging me to stay.' I said.

'Well I'm not any more. This is where this shit ends. If you do it again…' she trailed off.

'I take it you don't want to come travelling any longer,' I said.

She sighed, theatrically.

'It's getting to the stage that I'm not even sure we can be flatmates.'

'This is all because of Mark isn't it?' I said. 'I thought that was just a drunken one-off.'

'Whatever gave you that idea?'

In the darkness I rolled my eyes. She pulled my door closed behind her but it reopened a crack, the way it does. I heard her going to her room, then her key turning in the lock.

I watched the crack of light coming through the door and thought of her tattoo, of the sentences that, like threads bound briefly together at a point, converged with the word on her back, of all the stories that spiralled out from these sentences, unsaid, unread. Almost infinite.

From Lima, Rio and La Paz I sent her postcards. Our usual joke greeting each time.

Dear Donna,

Weather is here.

Wish you were beautiful.

Suzie.

But I wasn't sure, any more, how she would take the humour.

When I came back, I got a job and rented an apartment. Although Mark mentioned she wanted me to get in touch I waited three or four weeks before I called her.

A week later she sat on my sofa.

'Nice place,' she said.

'I could do with more furniture.'

'I guess.'

I looked closer at her. 'Are you wearing make-up?'

She blushed. 'So what if I am?'

'Oh, no reason, I always thought that you looked great without any.'

'Well, you know, I thought I'd give it a go tonight.' She pulled her cigarettes from her pocket. 'Mind if I smoke?'

I shrugged. 'There'll be smoke pouring out of the kitchen any minute now, so I can hardly object if you light up a fag now can I?'

She held out the box to me, and I took one.

'I swear you are trying to get me addicted.'

She raised her hands. 'You got me. Philip Morris has paid me a fortune to make sure you get hooked.'

'Well you're doing a good job.'

'That reminds me,' she said. 'You'll like this story. There was a comedian on the radio this morning. He was telling about how a year ago he had started to go out with a really good-looking girl. He knew, from the very start, that she was out of his league. It was only a matter of time before she dumped him for a better-looking guy. So he made a plan. He went out to a pharmacy and bought all their stock of nicotine patches. Every night after they made love and she had fallen asleep he would cover her body with these patches, and every morning he would be sure to wake before her, and gently take them off again.

After a while, just as he predicted, she hooked up with a lean, tanned lawyer, rich and perfect in every way. But the comedian was unfazed; he just waited. Sure enough she came back to him a few weeks later, a little confused.

"I don't know why," she said, "but every night I get these cravings to be in your bed…"'

I laughed.

'That's not a bad idea,' I said.

'I think it should be the basis of any successful relationship.'

'Addiction?'

'Sure.'

She was staring at me intently, her large brown eyes glittering. I wanted to throw myself on her right then and there.

'Did you miss me?' she asked.

'Only slightly.'

I went to the kitchen to check on the fish.

Afterwards we were on the balcony; I was leaning against the railing, looking down at the street below. She stood beside me, started to rub my back, up and down, long strokes.

'So South America was good?'

I shrugged. 'There are a million photos on my computer if you want the blow-by-blow account.'

She laughed. 'I'm okay thanks.' Then went to get another bottle of wine.

It got cold and we moved inside, sat on the sofa.

'You know that tattoo you have?' I asked.

She looked up, face blank. 'Hmmm?'

'The tattoo that you had on your back. What's the story with it?'

'I don't have a tattoo on my back.'

'I'm sure you do.'

'What of?'

'Just a word. "cleave" I think it is.'

'Nope, I'm afraid not. Perhaps you are thinking of someone else.'

She looked away. I shook my head, poured us more wine. She moved, lay her head on my lap.

My bed was small, and we lay side by side, skin on skin. In the darkness I tried to work out what it was that bound us together, trying to find, in her features, an indication of what she thought. But her face was smooth, open and blank. Her skin was just skin, her eyes were just eyes. There were no deeper truths to be read. Her breath mingled with mine and she leaned her head back to get some fresh air.

Later, as she was leaving, she bent to pick up her bag and I saw it again, where I knew it would be.

'There it is,' I said, touching it.

'What?' she said, trying to look over her shoulder. 'Is there something on me?'

'The tattoo, remember, I asked you about it earlier.'

'Oh,' she said. 'THAT tattoo.' As if there were any others to confuse it with.

That night it struck me there was another reading of the word, one that wasn't so hard to pin down. The tattoo could just be what it was, stripped of meaning, just a mark on her back. And I thought of writing down our story, of building it from the empty word she carries around with her and seeing where it led.

I got a call from her the next day.

'Mark waited up for me last night.'

'Oh, I hope everything is all right.'

'You shouldn't have let that happen,' she said.

'What?'

'Last night.'

'I don't remember forcing you.'

'You just don't get it, do you?'

But I didn't know how to answer her.

It was at least another two months before I saw her again. I had gone to Hogan's to meet Fred, and saw Donna sitting in a corner reading a book, a mug of tea on the table in front of her. Something jumped violently inside me. I went over to her.

'Hello stranger,' I said.

She looked up.

'Oh. Hi.'

Her left eye was half-closed by a swelling above it; this glowed with the technicolor of bruising: reds, purples, greens and blues. The white of her eye was flecked with red.

'Christ, what happened to you?'

She looked confused.

'Your eye,' I said.

'Oh, nothing really.'

She pulled a wave of hair down to cover the wound, lifted her bag off the seat beside her and put it on her lap.

She smiled. 'It's good to see you. Got a few moments to kill?'

'Sure.'

I sat in the chair opposite her.

'So, any news?'

'It's Mark and I…' she began, but stopped when the lounge boy came over. I ordered and he left, but came back almost immediately with a bowl of peanuts. I smiled at Donna. She drank some tea; it looked milky, cold, like it had been sitting there a while.

'Go on.'

I couldn't stop looking at her black eye. It had a quality that was hard to grasp, at once a part of her face, and separate from it.

She raised her hand, gently prodded the bulging mess.

'It's ugly isn't it?'

'It'll go down I'm sure. Did Mark…'

'Oh, no. No it's not like that.' She laughed. 'Christ, Mark wouldn't hurt a fly. You know that. No, I got it from hockey.'

'Oh.'

'I know how it sounds. But it's the truth.'

'Well, you should be more careful.' I felt stupid, matronly, it was the wrong thing to have said and I knew it. Donna smiled a tight little smile.

'Where was I? Oh yes, I was going to tell you our news.' She looked down into the bag on her lap, rummaged deep inside it.

'Don't you hate this fucking law?' she produced a pack of cigarettes and looked out the window at the wet streets. 'Do you mind joining me outside?' Of course I knew what she was going to tell me, and I wanted to shake her, point out how obvious she was, the way she was drawing out the moment even though it was clear she wanted me to know more than anything.

'Let me guess,' I said. 'You're getting married aren't you?' I suppose there was a small part of me that expected her to laugh and wave it away.

'Is it weird? You were away for so long of course; you haven't seen how well things have been going.'

'Mark told me you were getting on well, but I never imagined.' She was waiting for me to say something. I remembered. 'Congratulations Donna. You must be so happy.'

She nodded, smiled broadly.

We got up, gathered our things.

I followed her out. As she walked her top rode up slightly and I watched the patch of skin it revealed, waiting to see her tattoo again. It appeared once, briefly. We stood under the awning, she held out the pack and I took a cigarette.

'Still trying to turn me to the dark side?'

'Smoking is the last true extreme sport, you should thank me.'

As she held the flame to the end of my cigarette I saw that her hand was shaking slightly.

I blew out my first lungful of smoke.

'Did he ever find out about, you know, you and me?' I asked.

'Who, Mark? NO. Christ no.' She took a shaky drag from her cigarette. Laughed. 'Jaysus, can you imagine?'

Just then I heard Fred behind me, her German accent sounding out above the conversations around me. 'Ah, there you are Suzie; I thought maybe I had been stood up.' She came up and slipped an arm around my waist. 'I thought we said to meet inside.' She looked down at Donna. 'Hello.'

I could feel my face reddening.

'Donna this is Fredericka. Fred, this is an old friend of mine, Donna.' I took a drag from my cigarette. 'Donna is engaged to my brother apparently.'

'You haf a brother? You never said.'

I wanted to point out that she had only known me for two weeks, but it wasn't the time. Donna winked at me, looked at her watch.

'Christ. I better dash.'

I met Mark at home the following weekend.

'I saw Donna the other day,' I said.

'Oh really.'

'She told me your news. Congratulations.'

'Cheers. It was, you know, about time I suppose.'

'So you got down on your knees and all that romantic stuff?'

'I suppose I might have.'

'She had quite the shiner; you didn't have to convince her did you?'

He laughed. 'I don't know who gave her that, some amateur; I always make sure only to hit her where the clothes will cover it.'

'That isn't funny Mark.'

'For fuck's sake, are you seriously asking me this? Lighten up; she got it playing hockey or mugging an old lady or something.'

'If I ever find out you've hurt her…'

'Christ Suzie, you're totally out of line here, you should know I'd never do anything like that.'

At their wedding I only talked to Donna very briefly, while she was dashing to the toilets between courses.

'You look gorgeous,' I said, because she did.

'As do you dahling.' She giggled, then leaned one hand on my shoulder and whispered conspiratorially in my ear.

'You know, this shouldn't change our thing.' Her breath was warm, and I could smell the traces of alcohol lifting off it. I suddenly felt angry with her, with the whole mess of it. I wanted to hear her admit it.

'Oh really, what thing is that exactly?' I asked.

She looked confused, hurt perhaps. But before she could reply her uncle, a great rolling yawn of a man, came over and started talking to her about how great the service was. I left, got a glass of whiskey and sat with a group of her friends who were talking about the houses they couldn't afford. Mark stood up, started to make his speech. I let the words blur past me until, suddenly, I heard him saying my name.

'And a big thanks to my little sister Suzie for bringing Donna into my life.' He beamed at me, swaying slightly. Donna, I noticed, had the decency to look down at the table.

Christ, how long ago was that? My parents had been away and Donna and I were smoking a joint in my room, lying side by side. My mouth was still full of the taste of her, and my head was heavy with dope and tiredness. I went downstairs in my robe to get some water. Mark was there, having a beer and watching the TV. I leaned against the doorway and he looked up, smiled.

'Someone looks baked,' he said.

I grinned at him like the happy fucker I was.

'Maybe.'

'Got any to spare?'

'It's up in my room.'

Then I heard a sound behind me and I looked to my left and saw Donna coming down the stairs. She was wearing just her t-shirt and knickers, and I grimaced at her. She froze, mid-stride, and I could see she was trying to hold back some laughter.

'Who you got there?' asked Mark, and he stood up from the sofa and was in the hall too quickly for me to say anything. He looked up at Donna, who was still standing looking down at us.

'Hi,' she said.

'Oh. I'm sorry,' said Mark, 'I thought you had a guy over or something.' He kept looking at Donna, examining her, and she let him. I should have realised at the time, but I didn't. Donna got dressed and we all sat up late into the night, smoking and drinking.

At the end of Mark's speech everyone stood and raised their glasses with him.

I turned to the man beside me. 'It's enough,' I said, 'to put you right off ever sleeping with anyone isn't it?' He smiled, but I knew there was no way he could have got the joke.

'You want another drink?' he asked.

A year later I was in their house for a dinner. I had gone to the toilet. While there I had felt a sudden surge of panic, of fear. My hands clammed up and I stood with my hand on the door for a while. After I left I met Donna coming up the stairs.

'Can you come with me a second?' I asked her.

I took her back to the bathroom and locked the door. 'What's up with you?' she asked. I explained. I had found the lump two months before and had been ignoring it. I asked her if she thought I was imagining things or not.

'I need to know. Right now. I don't know why. It's driving me crazy. Can you check?'

'Christ Suzie. Do you ever fucking stop?'

I couldn't believe what she was saying.

'Do you honestly think that's what I'm doing here? Trying to seduce you? Think about it for a second Donna.'

But she left the room.

Later there was a knock on the door. It was Mark.

'You alright in there?'

'Never better. How the hell are you?'

I waited another four months before I went to get it checked out. The doctors were very honest with me, so I was scared into coming in straight away. In the hours after I woke I hadn't had the courage to look down at it. I had no need. Dried blood and the stubble of stitching no doubt. Orderlies came to me from time to time to change the tubes that ran in and out of it. 'To drain the lymph.' One told me. The liquid that was coming out was the colour of straw.

I was lying back, staring at the ceiling when I heard the sharp clack of heels approaching my bed. It was Donna, her belly domed forward with pregnancy. She sat down in the chair beside me, and breathed out the self-satisfied breath of the expectant mother.

We talked about nothing for a while, and then she got up, all agitated and worried, not like her at all. She came to my bedside and I saw the little lines on her face, and the red in her eyes. Christ, had she been crying? She leant over me, and I could smell her perfume, kind of a faint lemon and honey.

'I just wanted you to know,' she said, 'that you're not allowed give me any more scares like this one.'

I didn't know what to say to that so I changed the subject. 'Answer me one thing,' I said.

'Anything.'

I hadn't planned what to say next, and I thought of all the questions I had wanted to ask her down the years, and I realised that there was only one that I still cared to hear answered.

'That tattoo, when did you get it?'

'Oh, ages ago, back when I was in first year in university.'

'Funny tattoo to get.'

'Well I kind of had no choice in picking the word. It's part of a story.'

I pushed myself forward slightly in the bed.

'What's the story about?'

'Well, in truth, I don't know.'

'That sounds interesting.'

'I found out about it from an article in the college paper. An American artist who had written this two thousand word story, and wanted to have each word tattooed on a different person. She was looking for volunteers. I figured it sounded interesting. I wrote to her and about a month later got a card with the word on it. My instructions were to go out and get the tattoo and then send her back a photo of it.'

'And she never gave you a copy of the overall story?'

'Nope.'

'At least you got a good word. You know, not "the" or "and" or "I".'

'Thing is, those words would be fine, the truth is the word I have isn't quite the word I got.'

'No?'

'No, the word I got was 'eave'. You know, that timber part of the roof that joins it to the house. So I got the tattoo, and sent her the picture of the word she had asked for. But I wasn't going to go around with a word like that on me for the rest of my life. Happily I had a good idea. A few weeks later I went back and got the "c" and the "l" added. I've always liked that word, you know, how it has two meanings, both exactly the opposite to one another.'

'Yeah. I've always thought it suited you.'

'Thing is, I've always felt guilty about changing it.'

'Why?'

'I feel a bit like a vandal. The original story is dead now, isn't it? I guess I destroyed it.'

'I don't know. Hardly. Besides, there are always other stories for it to tell. For instance, one drunken night ages ago, when I couldn't sleep, I spent hours thinking up a story that started with your word.'

'Now that sounds like a story I would like to hear.'

She was looking me dead in the eyes. So close to me. Even though it was very sore to move them I raised my hands and I put them on her shoulders. We stayed like that for a while, but I knew that something more was required. I gritted my teeth to brace myself. The strange thing was that until my hands actually started to move I had no idea whether I was going to push her away, or pull her close.

'This is where it ends,' I said.

Candle
Nicky O'Neill

Candle

Alfred Hitchcock's *Birds*. A young, fit Tippi Hedren in the shower, screaming as they come swooping down. Favourite film, that, favourite scene, sat in front of the telly, DVD on, can of Special Brew in one hand and my pet snake in the other. I've got a boa constrictor named Bert. He likes the film too, or so it seems, anyway. He shed his skin once, just looking at it. I like Tippi, Bert likes her persecutors. Something for everyone in my house, that's how we live.

How we *used* to live. Jesus, the mess I'm in now, even Bert will have to go. Can't bear him near me any more. Eyes too shiny, like the telly when it's off. Like the patent leather shoes I bought when Stella said she'd see me that time.

I'd scream if I thought anyone could hear me.

Two months ago, a blazing July, stuck in the pee-stenching old people's home on a fiver an hour. A bit of a booze habit, a bit of a dope habit, nothing out of hand, just something to get a lad through the day. A lad with no wife and no future, with half his face blown away in that nightclub bombing twelve years ago. Some think they only invented terrorists on 9/11.

Rewind twelve years. There was me in shiny shoes, weekend pass. My birthday. *Twenty-one today, you've got the key to the door.* The locals kept their distance. There were a few troublemakers, but with a load of pissed-up squaddies in the place, it would've been suicide to try anything. Stella was there, I was on a promise.

When it blew, I was ordering her a *Red Witch*. I remember her explaining it to me: vodka and Pernod and blackcurrant. It'd make me throw up now. Can't bear the smell of Pernod after that night. She grinned that goofy grin of hers, teeth all crooked, mouth all sexy, her eyes all black in the underground light of the club. 'Maybe try a bit of magic on you, later,' she whispered, kissing my nose. I licked her earlobe. Some crappy love song was playing. I turned my back on her for a second and boom.

Lying in hospital, they came and asked me questions. Had I seen anyone acting suspiciously? Did I know my mates were all dead? Was I with anyone?

Of course I was with someone, the woman I might have married. Okay, I'd just met her but you don't know, do you? We might have gone up the aisle, had three kids, been off to RELATE by now. We might only have seen each other twice. She might have taken me back to her place and screwed me senseless. Or I might have come home and married Elaine, the girl I'd been seeing since I was a kid. I might have left the army, got a civvy job, something normal, insurance maybe. Men have drowned in lakes shallower than my self-pity.

I spent the best part of the next two years in hospital. They fixed me up as best they could but my face looked like it was made from melted wax. I only had one eye, one ear. No hair, eyelashes or eyebrows, just shiny skin stretched across my skull. Kids stared, laughed; occasionally they cried in terror. Most adults looked away. I became ageless, sexless, thrust into a premature twilight zone. For months I needed a zimmer. I was catheterised, got infections in my John Thomas every week or so. My right foot was missing when they found me so I had a prosthetic one fitted, moulded plastic, the colour of *Caramac*, but too dark for me – I was a ginner even without the hair. Mam looked after me, once the hospital could do no more. Back in the small bedroom in her semi, I stared at my old pictures of Nirvana and 808 State. The pictures of me and Elaine in Ibiza, I threw away. She came visiting, Elaine. Bunch of grapes with her. *Grapes*, for pity's sake. I could see she didn't want to look at me. The reek of death was too powerful, too poisonous. I might have contaminated her. She couldn't, wouldn't look at the dripping raw redness that was my skin. She left. Married a lad who worked in the local garage.

After that, no more women. I could walk, I could talk. I languished on the sick for a while and then in poorly paid jobs, sweeping floors, stacking shelves. I moved away from home to a new city and anonymity. I bought a boa, Bertie boy, and began to feel invulnerable.

My new job was in a care home. Depressing, filthy work at times, but at others, a great joy and a solace. With the work came Marianne, Senior Carer, my superior, who was loud and brash and laughed a lot. She joked with the ancient inmates. She joked around with me, told me all about herself. How she was my age, divorced, with two kids who spent every other weekend with their father. How she had psoriasis like her dad, making her skin break into deep red weals, all up her arms and legs. Soiled goods, she called herself, just like me. She called me *The Candle*. She asked if my John Thomas was burned as well, if it was the colour of molten wax. She grabbed my crotch as she said it. She looked a bit like Tippi, but fatter, more homely. Me and Bert sat and watched that film night after night, looking out for any clue in Tippie that would help me get closer to Marianne. John Thomas was still in working order but she would never get past my face to find out.

Gabrielle

The boy was curious. *Melted Boy*, they called him, *Candle*. I did not know then what had happened to his poor face. Drip, his skin went, down his nose. His left eye had been dragged, half-closed down his cheek. Melted boy had no mouth, only teeth, yellowed, tobacco-stained teeth, and a protruding tongue. Raw hands with bitten stumps for finger nails. His gait was clumsy. One foot, his left, his *sinister*, being placed so firmly upon *terra firma* I deduced it must be artificial. Melted Boy. He was so gracious, his one pale eye begging for acceptance, yet defensive. Poor lamb. Only one fly in the ointment. The girl, Marianne, was in love with the idea of saving him. All this I could see. This was the place. I sent for Mama.

Mama did not like the heat of the house. It was time for her mantle to be shed. It itched her, now, felt large and heavy. Warm June, the sickly stench of tea roses seeping through her open window, the radiators belching hot air, swirling dust motes around a room, the colour of sepia, as though it were already confined to history. Melted Boy came at my request. He knelt on the floor beside Mama and allowed her to finger his poor dripping skin. No longer sighted, her marbled eyes gazed inward. Her hands, clawed and bent though they were, traced the pattern of his life. Smoke from her cigarette wreathed around them. As they grew close, his curiosity found voice. I visited daily and often I would find him crouched at her knee, talking avidly. He would silence himself when I entered, or act the goat when the girl, Marianne, came in with her batteries of medication, her tea, her soothing banter, her growing love for her Candle. We would have to act quickly, this much I could see.

A Sunday afternoon: the sun was streaming onto Mama's head, Melted Boy's one eye leaked water in the excess of light. The room bloated with the stench of urine and old food and lavender talcum. He was looking hard at Mama, touching her temple in wonder. She indicated for me to show him her secret, to *explain.* I was afraid, suddenly. All my life I had lived with this truth, imparted it to no one. Now it must be given away. I took his stumpy hands in my own and began.

I noticed strangers staring, once I was passed puberty, into my twenties and thirties. Every time I was with Mama, I could see it in their faces. *That woman looks older than her own mother*, they would whisper. And indeed it was true. Well into old age, Mama's skin was unlined, plump and supple with the pinkish glow of youth. At seventy, she looked barely twenty. Only her eyes could give her away, and her slowly bending skeleton, clawing, powdering, as she crept toward senility. Poor beautiful Mama and her terrible secret.

Melted Boy would not, could not understand. He sat upon Mama's floor, confused. In me, he saw a wizened crone, purporting to be the offspring of a beauty. Though it was Mama's mind that had gone, and her bones that had crumbled, he glared at the crevices in my face, its lines and bags and wrinkles, and it was my sanity about which he drew conclusions. The sun beat into the room and Mama's breath grew faint.

From a local bookshop, I purchased a *Memoire* of Honoré Fragonard – not the girl-on-the-swing painter of chocolate-box sensuality, but the master of *ecorché*, an artist in his own right, still exhibited at the *Ecole Vétérinaire* in Paris, two centuries after his death. I taught Melted Boy about flaying, with the help of the book, demonstrated how the dermis and epidermis can be removed from a recently deceased body to expose nerves and sinew and blood vessels and bone, how this can be injected with wax to demonstrate vascular structure or muscle function. As he browsed the glossy pages illustrated with high-quality photographs of Fragonard's completed works, the Candle's eyes glowed. Repeatedly, he touched his own destroyed face. He perused the description of the flayed rider, sitting tall upon her horse. He fingered the pages of reptiles, stripped and posed as they would never be seen in life.

'What has this to do with me?' His first words were directed at me. Usually he spoke only to Mama. I believe my withered appearance nauseated him.

Mama whimpered. Gently, I pushed her hunched shoulders away from the chair back. I unzipped her dress and slipped it down to expose her youthful breasts and white shoulders. Melted Boy looked unhappy. It was down to him and the other carers to dress and undress those elderly people in their care, not a relative, not a daughter.

Mama's back was smooth, the colour of alabaster, but from her nape to her buttocks, a red scar could be traced, slightly raised. You could feel the bumps where the stitches were put in. I took his hand, encouraged his fingers to run the length of the scar. This he did, an expression of fascination transfixed upon his broken face. I took my scissors and began to snip. Melted Boy, awakening from his trance, cried out and lunged at me.

And then, Marianne walked in without knocking. That girl has sixth sense, I swear it. With her wily eyes, she took in the old woman crouched, the blade of the scissors, and Melted Boy's stumpy hands attacking my eyes. She ran towards us and knocked the scissors to the floor.

Marianne

I took the book home, the one the old biddy were on about Candle reading. It were full of weird stuff. Right weird. All birds and animals and people with no skin on. Bloody funny thing to give to anyone, I think, never mind a lad with a face half burned off. Candle were right upset by the carry-on with the scissors. Police had to be called and everything. The old woman who said she were the daughter were taken away.

I came across the story the night my eldest, Sean, got chickenpox. He had a temperature of over a hundred and I couldn't sleep, for thinking he might die. So I sat there by his bed, staring at the book, trying to take my mind off things.

When Honoré Fragonard's fiancée died from consumption, he were said to be broken hearted. They had the funeral and burial and everything and then someone went and nicked the body out of the grave. Weird, eh? But it was the seventeen hundreds so people were up to all sorts. Anyway, next thing they knew this bloody great horse and rider effort appears in Honoré's studio. Both had been skinned. Apparently you can still see them in some weirdo museum in Paris. Honoré had already made quite a name for himself for being able to remove the skin from animals. *Ecorchés* they call them. Trouble was, no one knew where he'd got this new body from and what with the grave robbery, conclusions were drawn. But, according to the story, something else was wrong. The skin he took off his beloved after cutting her from top to bottom was perfect. Like a suit, it was said, and anyone who fitted could have put it on. This was all hush hush, mind, and for years no one knew about this skin suit except Honoré's brother who found it hanging up in a cupboard.

So, the brother steals the skin and wonders what to do with it. It happened that a few years previous, his wife had had a dose of the pox and her boat-race looked like some cobbled street in the centre of Paris. Apparently the brother made her wear a veil so no one could see how hideous she looked. So the brother asked Honoré if he could put the skin suit over his wife's ugly mug. Honoré was only too glad to help and the experiment was done. They skinned, or as it says in the book, *flayed* the wife and dressed her up fine and dandy in the new skin. Straight away it grew onto her body, making her look young and lovely again, no pock marks, no scars. So everyone was happy.

The tale fizzles out after that, though there is some hint there was more to come. The wife's new skin never aged, so it said, and when she was dying, *madam bequeathed the mantle to her eldest daughter*. It kind of made me wonder. I couldn't stop thinking of Candle and his dripping skin, of the red sores up my arms, of the old woman with a seam up her back. And my son, lying there, his face covered in blisters that oozed and itched. At least he would get better.

Next day, I were on an early. Our Sean were on the mend so I took him round to his dad's. I couldn't afford to lose the shift money. First thing I did was go into the old woman's room. Anna, her name was, short for something foreign-sounding. She was Russian, according to the notes, family all shot in the Revolution. Candle had beaten me to it. He were bent over the old woman, who was lain on her bed on one side. He'd pulled her nightie up to reveal the long railway-track scar her daughter had tried to cut open. I were just about to moan on and ask him what he were doing and wouldn't it be better if he emptied her commode, when it all began to make sense. Well, not sense, but some kind of story. A *mantle*, they'd called it and old Anna had a seam right up her body. We checked the inside of her legs and arms and found seams there, too. Another thing, the skin were too big. Not like old people's normally is, when it gets all loose and baggy. It was like a thick overcoat whose owner had shrunk. I told Candle what I'd read.

'You are joking,' he said, touching his face, his poor melted face. I wanted to kiss him then.

'No.' I pulled the book out of my tabard pocket. 'Read that part. It's what they did back then. I think the old woman was trying to tell you something. You can get a new skin, a new face. You can be *whole* again.'

His one working eye was full of water as he looked up from the book.

'You really think?' he said, gazing at me.

'I'll help you,' I promised.

Candle

The skin retains a memory deeper than any scar, more grotesque than the melted mass that was my face. It slipped over my flayed torso, over my broken face, like a new suit, 'a birthday suit', Marianne joked, though this was no joking matter. Blood and gore, an old woman dying. Me shivering, pulsating, my eye hanging on my cheek. Honoré Fragonard's book of instruction lay between us on the bed table. Marianne had brought surgical scissors and she wore a surgeon's mask. The cut was deep, the peeling excruciating. She set about my flaying with humour and determination, pouring vodka down my neck as she did so. Anna's skin was so much easier. It was no longer attached to her body, but came away easily, ready to be taken by a new owner. Anna lay moaning on the bed. She was dying but I knew we were doing the right thing. We had discussed what to do. Her death would appear natural; a burning cigarette. I kept my faith in Marianne, in Honoré Fragonard's skill, in the immortal quality of the epidermis I was to assume.

The new skin didn't feel as I had expected. Like a suit of armour, it sat over my flayed body, heavy and stiff. I closed my eyes, knowing my agonies to be over.

Then I heard a scream, a kind of scritching, scuttling noise. Marianne set up a caterwauling such as you've never heard. With immense difficulty, I focussed my one eye. The new lid felt like the crisp dead carapace of some long dead insect. I saw a blur of red. Anna, the dying woman, the creature on the bed, was flying at Marianne. Red and raw. This creature was flying like a demented bat at a window. Marianne was holding my own dripping skin. The fat below the dermis from gut and buttocks looked like lumps of yellow lard. The empty skin of my John Thomas hung withered as an abandoned condom. The dying creature clawed at this skin. I could see the movement of her skeleton, her muscles, the blood coursing through her veins. She grabbed my skin from Marianne's grasp and began to put it on. I swear. Like a dress, a coat. First head, then body, slipping in her legs like a pair of stockings. She stood there, this thing, triumphant. She died in the fire we set.

I am not a snake. My new skin hasn't grown naturally over my body. My new skin is the hardened remains of a score of lives, lives lived in the dark. Those possessors of this skin, this dermis which moulds so magnificently to whatever form lies beneath, wasted years seeking the very state in which I find myself, and the remainder of their lives trying to escape. This monstrous skin retains the echoes of their terror, the beat of their burnings and searings and flayings. Beautiful I may be, but I am possessed by pain, unable to contemplate my own reflection.

Last night, Marianne visited. It is rare she leaves her own house, assailed as she is by visions of the old woman's last moments. Her skin is vivid with red weals. We could not bear to touch each other; contented ourselves with sitting side by side on the sofa watching Tippi Hedren in *The Birds*.

Tick-Bite Precautions

Diane Cockburn

The Disease Comes in Various Forms

I am on the rough patch of grass outside our cottage, watching the midges crawling on your neck. They are in a thick cloud around you and they are biting. I can see tiny probosces spearing your skin. I am covered in 'Jungle formula' and have my cagoule tightly laced around my chin. The water is running off us as we stand looking out over the loch. The ferns drip drip with the drizzle. I look at your midge-encrusted face and notice the rhododendrons are all enormous leaves with no flowers. They would have been scarlet if we had come in May.

We are watching for sea otters. We do this every evening after tinned tomato soup and toast. Five more days to go. A seal swims past. I point. You say, 'Oh, yes.' Your teeth are quite yellow. Suddenly we see the stream of bubbles out beyond the rocks. The loch is black with peat. An otter slides over and under the water, whiskers dripping, and eyes reflecting the dark, its fur slick and damp. It dives and disappears. I finger the 'after bite' in my pocket and do not reveal its whereabouts.

Yesterday we walked to the ruined schoolhouse on the other side of the island. You made cheese sandwiches and a flask of sweetened tea. I do not take sugar. We stopped by the broken boating pond and startled a deer grazing on the overgrown terrace. It bounded away and I took a few steps to follow it down the path, which led to the 'honeymoon cottage' mentioned in the brochure. You said, 'Don't go there.' You said, 'It will rain soon.'

The sea otter floats on its back, a misshapen mussel on its stomach. It is hitting the mussel hard with a rock. The sound echoes over the loch.

'Whack! Whack! Whack!' The otter keeps pounding the rock onto the mussel. There are ticks everywhere, even though we can't see them. You make me carry out tick-bite precautions. There is greenness, deep water, stones, and mud. There is the stink of rotting seaweed. We have read all the books on the bookshelf. There is no reception on the communal cabin TV. Someone has written 'what a rip' on the blackboard and smashed the only ping-pong ball. You think this is hilarious.

We are watching the otter crush the shell and pull out thin strands of living mussel flesh. It is making crunching noises and its whiskers hang down long and loose. When it has finished it will roll over and its supper will just be washed away. Then it will dive down deep into the black loch waters leaving nothing but a trail of silver bubbles.

Inspect Skin Regularly

Tonight is tick-hunting night. After the tweezers broke it hardly seemed worth the trouble, but we take it in turns to strip down to underwear and lie on the bed. Our leaflet says Lyme disease starts with a ring-shaped rash on the face. It is hard to see by the light of the torch but you say it is easier to pluck ticks off in the dark. We are playing a dangerous game. I missed one yesterday and today it is still there on your stomach, fat as a puffball. I change the subject before the battery runs out. The night attaches itself to the corners of the room and then leaps over everything, rubbing out the last chance of tick picking. No moon. I lie down on my army blanket bed, listening for the tiny lapping as your tick feeds, sticking its barbed mouthparts into the warm folds of your skin.

Wear Light Clothing to Make the Ticks More Visible

I have met a man in a yellow cagoule laced up tight like mine by the jetty when you were still asleep and I wanted to book the rowing boat for the day and you said I should go and see the ferryman first thing in the morning while you got the breakfast ready. His cagoule is slick and shiny. I think it is made of oilskin and he does not appear bitten. I think he has supplies of something exciting, perhaps chocolate.

Wear Closed Shoes or Boots with Trousers Tucked into Boots

I have one on my thigh. I don't think you have seen it as when we went for that walk yesterday you told me not to wear those shorts and I laughed and said I was going to walk near the bracken not through it, but I didn't notice the track all overgrown and was too busy feeling sorry for that tethered horse in the clearing. It was covered with tiny spidery bodies and its flanks were quivering. Ticks climb to the top of blades of grass and wait for you to brush against them because our bodies are hot and they think 'Ahah! A fat deer!' and they latch on in a mad latching frenzy. I was running down the path screaming and tearing at my legs and you said nothing, just had that smile which said 'my trousers are tucked firmly into my boots thank you very much and you wouldn't catch me taking off my thermal socks and I knew those sandals were a stupid idea'.

Spray Clothing with Permethrin, which Repels Ticks

I am wearing perfume. I bought it in that tiny gift shop when I went over to the mainland to buy some milk and the papers. The man in the cagoule noticed it straight away and told me he liked a good scrub with carbolic soap every morning and a dip in the loch, weather permitting. He then rubbed his hand up my knee and offered me a fruit pastille. It was strawberry flavour and was next to my favourite coloured orange one next in the tube.

Check Your Entire Body

I am going swimming with the man in the cagoule. He says to meet him on the jetty at dawn and I am here. It is freezing and it is drizzling and it is too early in the morning. You are snoring on your back and your tick has dropped off. I find it on the floor all fat and blood-drunk under the bed and stamp on it. When I get here he is wearing a pair of orange rubber shoes and nothing else. He says jump in, you don't need a swimsuit, but I am wearing my lycra with reinforced gusset. Under the cagoule he is not quite what I was expecting. Kind of shrivelled and his arms look like giant peanuts.

To Remove a Tick Use Fine Tweezers, Grasp it Close to the Skin and Pull Firmly Away; Clean with Antiseptic

I walk slowly down the jetty, noticing how the planks pluck at my feet. He is already in and is blowing out water through his mouth and nose with great snorts. He is grinning and splashing. He smells of antiseptic.

I jump off the end, and then I swallow great gulps of dark peaty water. It smacks me in the face and I sink down. Kicking hard I see my arms all stained with juice. He must swim here a lot. I don't want arms like peanuts. Under the water it is completely black. 'Ahah!' he shouts as he surfaces and lunges at me in awkward grabs. He is trying to latch on. His lips are sucking at my shoulder and his hands are on me. I laugh and cuddle in to him, but then with a big kick I push him away with my strong feet. He kind of howls in an angry way and I know there is no chance of any more sweets. I decide never to buy you any rubber shoes.

Retain the Tick and Seek Advice on Additional Measures

I am swimming on my back, kicking strongly. I am used to the cold water now and it feels icy. He has dived down again and I can see him under the water amongst the seaweed bladders, just like a big bladder himself, all swollen up and his face like a pickled onion in malt vinegar. I swim away and out of danger into the deeper water. I cannot see him and wait for him to burst out beside me with his big arms all pawing at me. He does not come up.

This does not worry me as he is a natural swimmer and probably has swum off after some other fragrant person in a cagoule. He is a bog man, at home in the peaty water, slowly pickling away until someone finds him many centuries in the future and marvels at his perfectly preserved skin and lips parted to whisper something profound. Perhaps he is a primitive sacrifice to the gods, his rubber shoes part of the ritual, representing the finest craftsmanship of his time. I wonder if there are water ticks and will they suck him and suck him until he is all skin. I think I will give our things a good soaking in the sink and tomorrow we will hire the boat and go fishing on the other side of the island. I think I shall take the lock off the suitcase and allow you free rein with my selection of medical products.

Seek Vaccination, Ideally a Month in Advance if You Are Travelling in Dangerous Areas

I swim to the side and climb out. He has left his things in a neat heap and I stroke the cagoule a little. It would feel good on me. I slip it on as neat as a skin and it is all squeaky and yellow. The pockets are bulging with interesting shapes. He has a large bar of carbolic soap, which might come in handy. I imagine you in orange rubber shoes, in a swimsuit made from tick bites. He has a new pair of tweezers. I imagine us latching on to each other on blades of grass.

We stand on the rough ground outside our cottage and watch the midges gathering in drifts under the rhododendron bush. I am wearing a yellow cagoule laced around my chin and you have a ring-shaped rash.

Part II
Skin

Morphea

Katy Massey

I was eighteen and my brother Paul had been dead two years when I first noticed the disease curling itself, serpent-like, around my right side. It seemed to appear overnight: a raised opaque dark brown welt standing proud against my yellow-copper skin. The marking started at the side of my ribs and crept forward underneath my right breast.

I didn't hate my scar; it was my companion, a familiar whose condition more often than not reflected my own. The months passed and the mark grew darker in hue, from opaque brown to burnt umber, and the edges feathered into a mottled pocking, its sharp rim blurred and the line dissolved between the scar and my flesh. As the months drew into years the darker areas began to get that same tortoiseshell appearance and softened a little – some of the thick-ridged toughness of flesh, like a band of cartilage reaching under my breast, had, it seemed, worn away.

I had no idea what it could be and eventually visited the doctor to rule out skin cancer, the risk of which was just beginning to be publicised. Dr Butt ruled out cancer but suggested I might be allergic to elastic, as the spreading weal (by now about ten inches long by three inches wide) vaguely followed the line of the bottom of my bra strap and lower cup. Instinctively I ruled this out. If this was the case, why not a knicker-shaped pattern on my torso? Also, at size 36E, giving up bras simply wasn't an option. I would rather live with the intruder. From then on, every trip to see a new doctor was marked by my asking if they'd seen anything like it before. Each tried an off-the-cuff diagnosis. 'It's a keloid,' or, 'Are you using a different soap powder?' or, 'You should see some of the things I get in the surgery'. This last followed a disapproving tut-tutting at my evident vanity and self-obsession. I wonder now why I wasn't more bothered by the mark, but as medical professionals were generally dismissive, perhaps I grew dismissive too. As if to pay the scar attention was to somehow validate it. Or perhaps it was better to minimise the problem simply because they couldn't diagnose it. If they didn't understand it then it couldn't be serious, could it?

In the following years I learned a little about my scar. I learned that it didn't snake over my side but snaked over my 'flank', because in language, a person's 'side' is the same as a horse's. I learned that it changed, but so, so slowly that you'd have to have been me to notice. During one memorable phase it became a deep calm violet and must have been thinning, as it was almost translucent. I could see my normal skin beneath it like a thunderous sky through a dirty net curtain, and I thought the marking was finally deserting me. But then the tissue toughened and closed over again, and the prettier violet was replaced by the hardened umber brand I had started with.

I learned also that at times of stress or excitement it would become active. It would itch slightly; it stung like excitable pins and needles and burned like the nettles did when I played out as a child. During these periods the welt turned red and irritated and flakes of skin would peel off like forgotten shames, revealing more bark-like tissue beneath.

I had thought the scar would be my constant, inexplicable branding, a mysterious unfolding narrative on the collision of memory, pigment and flesh. But when I was in my mid-twenties I noticed a large patch of darkening skin on the front of my left thigh, like a large bruise. I had no notion until then that the umber marking was part of a syndrome or complaint. I had thought it was personal, unique to me. It had after all been inexplicable, so I had explained it to myself. But a companion marking meant a pattern was being established. It scared me. What next? A port wine stain on my cheek? And would anyone listen if one did appear? So again I went to the doctor, but this time I stood my ground (or rather sat stolidly in the municipal chair by his desk) until I had secured a precious referral to a consultant.

After a long wait for the appointment I met Dr Whittaker, dermatologist at the Royal Free Hospital in Hampstead. He took a close interest in my marks. First he asked me to undress to the knickers and sit up on one of those high metal beds that are always in consulting rooms. He handed me a towel to cover my modesty. When he asked me to let the towel drop, I did, trusting in his professionalism and the many witnesses – a gaggle of medical students – he had brought with him. Then he picked up my heavy breasts in both of his hands and hoiked them as high as he could before letting them drop. They rebounded a few times in a dancy, uneven way as if taking advantage of the opportunity for excercise. Dr Whittaker's face was a couple of inches from my chest and his head bobbed up and down in time with my breasts as they came to rest. Mortified, I could hear only the rushing of blood in my ears, and tried my hardest to disassociate my brain from everything happening from the neck down.

Because of my temporary deafness I've no idea why he did this – I have come to think it was so he could establish that there was no difference in weight between the breast afflicted with the strange markings and the other, unblemished one. However, he seemed pleased that he'd got the result he was looking for and after handing me my towel back, briskly informed me that he would schedule a biopsy on my thigh. This turned out to be a painless and humiliation-free procedure where a sliver of scar tissue was removed from the mottled, thickened flesh on my thigh.

A couple of weeks later and several years after the first mark appeared I finally had a diagnosis: **mor · phe · a** (môr-f) *n.* A localized form of scleroderma characterized by hardened, slightly depressed patches of dermal fibrous tissue. Also called *circumscribed scleroderma, localized scleroderma.* (*Stedman's Medical Dictionary*, 2nd Edition, 2004)

You will find this definition on the internet. You will also find that morphea is an autoimmune condition that results in the overproduction of collagen which forms into tough patches of scar tissue. In my case it's fairly benign, except that new patches will appear and disappear randomly. Most importantly you will read that no proven effective treatments for morphea exist. It was suggested to me that some positive outcomes had resulted from taking Larium, an anti-malarial drug which carries a risk of triggering psychotic episodes. I demurred, relieved that after all the hospital visits everything had turned out as I had thought it would. I simply had to live with the condition. It would get on with its life cycle as I got on with my life. Fortunately, I had already learned to do that.

It also turned out that I had been quite lucky. A much less benign form of the condition affects the muscles and joints causing aches and pains, carpal tunnel syndrome, and limbs to waste away or, in children, growth failure.

I looked a little harder at the various medical websites and read that morphea is rarer in dark-skinned individuals than Caucasians, on whose skin it presents as pink-ivory in appearance. Being mixed-race, it seems I had inherited more of a propensity for the disease from my Canadian mother, but that the dark skin bequeathed by my Jamaican father was responsible for the unusual appearance of the condition on my flesh: a kaleidoscopic range of blackness from bruise-purple to tortoiseshell to bitter chocolate.

After twenty years I have reached accommodation with morphea. I feel like a benign host to the condition, though occasionally I'll wake in the night with a noose of sheets around my neck as I've fought unconsciously to avoid the burning in my flank or thigh. Eventually, the disease may literally burn itself out but the life cycle of the condition may be decades and I am too used to it to passionately desire it gone. Morphea is a part of me now – a peculiar presence on my skin because of the particular mix of blood I have. The way my morphea looks is a mark of miscegenation, a mild disfigurement which has in some way figured me and I wouldn't be without it.

My Skin, Us

Rochita Loenen-Ruiz

Where I come from, skin is important. Let me correct that – skin colour is important.

In a country populated by brown – to dark-skinned – people, milky white is the ideal colour. It proclaims to the world that you are either the daughter of a rich man or a mestiza. While we carry umbrellas to shield our skin from the sun, pale skinned tourists unveil nubile bodies to welcome its rays. On white sand beaches, we watch them roast. First they turn pinkish, change from pale almost ghostly white to lobster red, and if lucky they arise from our beaches with tanned bodies. Brown – the ideal colour of the new European.

'Look at them,' we say to one another.

We bask in their praise of our latte-coloured skin, proclaiming a gospel of 'brown is beautiful'. It's a gospel we ourselves do not believe.

When I was younger, we all wanted to be white. I remember Ate Connie sitting for hours in the bathroom, soaked in a mysterious mixture of petroleum jelly, bleach and some other cream while the rest of us knocked on the door and begged to be let in.

Ate Connie just sat there and we had to wait until the required number of hours had passed before she came out. She'd run upstairs, a towel wrapped around her waist, her hair in a bun and stand in front of the mirror staring at her body.

'Am I whiter?' she'd ask.

We didn't see any difference, but we nodded anyway.

After a few months her skin, which once gleamed like mahogany, was now covered with a fine film of white.

'And now?'

We nodded our heads.

'Yes, Ate Connie. Now, you're whiter.'

Later on, Ate Connie married a foreigner who loved the colour of her skin.

'Aw, don't go bleachin' your skin,' he'd say. 'I love you jes the way you are.'

She moved to America and that was the end of the long waiting lines at the bathroom door.

I married a European.

Here in this flat country, in this once upon a time paradise, the colour of my skin becomes a wall I bounce up against every time.

My son turned to me and said, 'Mama, you're a foreigner.'

'Why do you say that?' I asked him.

'Because your skin is brown, not white like mine and the others'.'

For the longest time, he was obsessed by skin colour. How Papa was white and I was brown and he was somewhere in between. His obsession passed and we moved on to other topics but the issue of skin and colour continued to haunt me.

Once, the Netherlands was called the land of the tolerant. When I came to live here, I imagined I'd found utopia. Skin colour didn't matter, race didn't matter, and how much money you had in the bank was not of consequence, because everyone was equal. It felt like a welcome change, to enter a land where my marriage to a foreigner was not looked upon with suspicion. No matter what people say about intercultural marriages being an accepted thing – where I come from, too many of us have married foreigners out of economics so that every mixed marriage is viewed with a mixture of scepticism and belief. The question always chases us behind our backs: 'Did she really marry him out of love?' I used to think that way too, until I fell in love with an absent-minded, pale-skinned European. So when we got off the plane, and I inhaled Dutch air for the first time, I felt I could throw off the shackles of an old society.

'We are all equal here,' we said to one another during the required language courses. We were a group of newcomers to the Netherlands, and we swallowed the gospel of tolerance and equality as if it were a decree from the Lord God himself. Our Paradise dream didn't last for long. These days, you can almost taste the tension simmering under the skin of Dutch society. Animosity as tangible as flesh – it's there in living colour. When you turn on the TV, when you read the papers and when you walk down the streets, you can feel eyes watching you.

'Foreigner. Go back to where you came from.'

These are the words they don't dare to mouth out loud. If you listen very closely though, you might hear them whisper these words behind the curtains of their houses. Perhaps I've lived here so long that some of them forget I am one of those foreigners, and so I get to hear the cutting remarks first hand. Speculations about the Moroccan down the street and how come he can afford to have two cars while a Dutchman can only afford one.

'Surely, he must be doing something illegal. You know how these allochtonen are.'

Speculations about people coming from third world countries.

'That girl marrying a man old enough to be her father. Obscene. These Asians will do anything to climb up out of their squalor.'

This last usually trails off when they remember where I came from, and they turn questioning eyes to me, as if asking me to affirm or reject their speculations.

I smile and drink my cup of tea before saying: 'Yes, it is true that some of us marry for economics, but a lot of us marry for love. And you'll notice Asian women are faithful wives.' I say this in a calm voice and don't say what I am thinking inside my head.

The way I see it, the colour of my skin or where I came from shouldn't matter.

'Aren't I more important than the colour of my skin?'

'You are,' my husband says. 'And I think your skin is beautiful.'

When we embrace, I think how in an ideal world, this is just how it should be. White embracing the brown, brown embracing the white, contrasting and complementing each other, and sometimes mingling so that we produce this wonderful colour of skin that is our child.

Not everyone agrees with my point of view. There are those who argue for racial purity. 'We're a tolerant country,' they'll say. 'Perhaps too tolerant.'

In this society, there are layers of politeness that won't let most of them say the words they are thinking. Nevertheless, the words they don't say feel like skin pulled taut over a can that's ready to explode. Underneath the surface, I can taste their hatred and their fear.

It's not really me they're afraid of, it's not really me they hate, but what I represent, I suppose. That's how all persecutions start, don't they? Like how the Egyptians persecuted the Israelites in the Old Testament, that was all born out of fear, wasn't it? Paranoia, wasn't it?

I remember reading sentences along the lines of: 'They'll overrun the country if we don't watch out.'

Of course, they don't do persecution in this country. Persecution. They frown on it, as if it were a curse word. That's what the word *Allochtoon* has become, some sort of curse word that represents the shape of our anonymous skin. A blanket spread over all of us who bear distinct marks of being non-Dutch.

When I walk into a store, I can see who judges me by the colour of my skin. I can see it in the woman who follows me around, trying to be discreet about checking whether I am going to pay for my purchase or not. I hear them talking about me. They think I can't hear, but their whispers are so loud, they penetrate even the hidden corners of the little shop.

'You can't trust these allochtoon people,' the shop lady says to the girl behind the pay counter. And she looks at me as if she can't see that I am one of those allochtoon she's talking about.

'I'm allochtoon,' I say to her.

'I don't mean you,' she replies.

Even so, I feel her eyes on my back, and I can almost hear her words bouncing off the surface of my skin.

Society's skin has grown thin as an onion peel. So thin, it will tear if you peel it off. They can't bear us being here, even as they acknowledge why we are here. Sometimes, I wonder how deep the judging and the hating goes. On some days, I think, 'Maybe it isn't as bad as I think it is.' Then I pick up the morning paper and there it is screaming at me, that word. *Allochtoon.* The word is a blanket that covers me in the anonymous skin that identifies us: outsiders. People who don't belong.

The Three and a Half Day Parent

James K Walker

Laurence Llewelyn Bowen is to Marriage What Salt is to a Slug

I gladly let her have the lot. I didn't need reminders; it was easier that way. I told her to come around while I was out and to take everything, and I meant, everything. When I returned there was nothing left, she had done exactly what I had asked. She was always good to the word and I suspect that was one of the problems of our relationship.

Upon the fitted kitchen worktop (which she surprisingly had not dismantled) was one knife, one fork, one cup and one plate. She didn't leave a spoon. She knew I hated spoons, it meant puddings and ice-cream and I wasn't into all that.

The items were arranged neatly on the worktop suggesting that a meal was on the way. There was no meal on the way but at least the cooker was still there. She hated that cooker and always complained that it only ever burnt the tops of pies whilst somehow failing to defrost their contents. I suppose I kind of felt like that cooker now, which I guess makes her the pie.

By the food was a note telling me she had taken everything. Even upon splitting up she failed to recognise me as a competent human being, doubting that I would not notice the sudden emptiness of the house or that I may have forgotten. Perhaps she thought I was in some kind of denial and would pretend that none of this was happening.

The note made me sad because she had even taken the pad and the pen with her, leaving a solitary sheet with scribble. She hadn't even bothered to write neatly. The note was one of those 'I'm not a racist but…' because it said she still loved me and then in the next sentence explained she had to go. She also said she had found someone else, someone who could put up shelves straight and didn't lose their drill. I attribute her no blame for giving in to such temptation. I reserve that for the influx of home decoration programmes which have invaded the living room. Our marriage never stood a chance once the leather-panted Llewelyn Bowen came on the scene.

I decided to throw the note in the bin because if I didn't I would only keep reading it over and over again. However I ended up keeping the note. My change of heart was not due to prosperity but because she had taken the bin as well. It was only one of those £5.99 plastic ones. It seems strange how love boils down to such ridiculous things.

I decided to make myself a coffee when I realised the kettle had gone as well. The Nescafe had followed in hot pursuit. I laughed, she was priceless, and then thought one last fuck would have been nice. Then I started to cry at our selfishness and how my sexual needs were no different to her uses for a £5.99 plastic bin. It was no wonder we were splitting up.

At least she had left me the fridge, although that was something else she never liked. She said it used to make a whining noise and it felt like there were people screaming in her head. I could never hear it. It wasn't that I didn't believe her it was just after a ten-hour shift of operating machines I couldn't hear anything else. In fact I was envious that she could even find metaphors within her torture. I opened the fridge to take a cold glass from the Brita water filter jug to quench my thirst, but that had gone also. It obviously didn't make a whining noise and now she had a new man it was his digestive system that must be purified if he is to remain healthy and rectify the shelves.

I decided to risk my health and put faith in the £453 yearly water rates I paid without complaint – and took a glass from the tap; cautiously allowing it to run for two minutes first. I was quickly learning not to take anything for granted and words of wisdom from my boss started to flood into my mind after years of blocking them out. 'When you assume you make an ASS out of U and ME.'

The water looked clear enough. I went to sit down, taking my first gulp of a wasted potential that could so easily have been purified or coffee in another life. Sadness was everywhere I looked. Sadness was also everywhere that I fell, which is exactly what happened when I crashed to the ground as the seat and dining table were no longer there.

My sole cup smashed, forcing its contents onto the floor. Instantaneously the clear liquid streamed into a line and headed for my knees as if still determined to enter my body. I had to admire its perseverance, the way it needed to find a place to rest as well. Then I started to laugh, although I think this was to disguise the fact that I was really crying. She was right. I am stupid, I don't take any notice. Even now I take it for granted that the chairs are still there when my eyes so clearly prove that they are not.

I never thought I was a bad person but perhaps I am. I wondered if she would find this all funny if she could see me now, would she tell me to watch the broken cup or had we entered that stage of a relationship where clumsy becomes stupid and forgetful becomes inconsiderate? There was no point dwelling on it too much as the point was, we didn't have a relationship, and the sooner I realised this the quicker I would stop breaking cups. There was one positive. I didn't need to go out and buy a mop because I had only spilt water and even though it hadn't been purified it wasn't going to stain the carpet.

I realised that now she had freed me of so many things I should remain naked for a little longer. In the future I would invest in paper plates and plastic cups and never worry again about buying wash-basins that match the wallpaper, or wood over chrome breadbins. I may even invest in paper pants. From now on I would only buy essential items like a fast boil kettle, an electric toothbrush, and a Brita water purifier.

I looked at the walls for comfort now I had no wife to turn to and I realised how bare they were. That she had taken all the pictures of our son with her. Was it not enough that she had him every day without looking at pictures as well? Obviously not. I missed those pictures of my son, stills from his life. The school race, the birthday parties and then I realised I had been working when they had happened and now the pictures were gone I didn't even have the pseudo-memories to turn to.

Leaving that house was easy…you have to when it is sold. I took all my possessions with me; my records that she never liked, my books that she never read, my clothes that she never chose and of course not forgetting the knife, fork and plate. The house was so desolate I kind of wished I did eat puddings, just to have found dignity in possessing and packing up a spoon. As I left the garden I turned around and took one last look above the gate. I could still see her in summer, playing with our son in the garden, hiding the action man in the plants that never grew and it was so real it scared me, like they were still there. My reverie was interrupted by the next-door neighbour who pulled up in his car with his music blaring, true to form. He slammed his door so everybody could hear him and stared at me as he walked past.

'Off then are you?'

'Yep.'

'Right you are then.' And off he walked, slamming the back door behind him so his girlfriend knew he was back. I felt completely insignificant, as if forced behind a two-way mirror in which you are only ever able to see out. For the first time in my life I was consciously aware of how nothing really matters and how ridiculous it all is. I also realised that I was a fool if I expected compassion off a neighbour when it is hard to even find this in friends. I put my stuff into the car, feeling genuinely thankful that I hadn't had to lug any heavy items down the stairs and prepared to find somewhere else to temporarily live. Perhaps Tracey Emin's tent is up for sale?

Just as I started up the engine my neighbour came crashing back through his gate, spreading himself across the bonnet of the car like I was under arrest. Too many reruns of *Starsky and Hutch* on Sky are to blame.

'I've still got your drill,' he begins, 'I borrowed it off your wife, ex-wife.'

I am quite shocked that she hasn't been around to collect it and figure that it must simply be because it is a smaller version than the one her new partner has got and so she no longer has use for it.

'It's okay, you can keep it…' but he interrupts, 'I know I can, you're wife said so. The problem is there are some drill bits missing. Have you got them?'

At first I think he is joking then I remember that this is not the kind of trait which is synonymous with his personality.

'They're in the garage,' I sigh, 'don't worry its unlocked.'

'Do you know whereabouts?'

'On the top shelf of the left wall next to some old tins of paint.'

'Can I have the paint as well?'

'Yes.'

'What colour is it?'

It is at this point I feel myself starting to get really angry but just when I think I am going to shout I start to laugh. I have about as much control over my emotions as I do with my life. Fortunately it is enough to scare my neighbour off, ex-neighbour as I finally say goodbye to this street.

Park Life

'Did it hurt when you had your eyebrow pierced?'

'No.'

'Bet it did.'

'It didn't.'

'Not just a little bit?'

'Well perhaps a little.'

'So it did hurt then?'

'Yes.'

'Why lie about it then?'

The word has spread far and yonder that a free babysitter is available and so I am looking after my friend's two boys. They are very clued up and inquisitive yet uninterested in the park.

'Have you ever had your nose pierced?'

'Yes.'

'I thought only punks had their nose pierced?'

'You've a lot to learn.'

'Were you a punk when you had it pierced?'

'No.'

'Well why did you have it done then?'

It's hard enough convincing yourself you have made an individual statement without justifying it to a child. They don't buy any of it such is the purity of their minds.

'Have you had your ear pierced?'

'Yes.'

'Does that hurt?'

'A little.'

'Does it hurt as much as your nose?'

'Or your eyebrow?' adds his brother.

'No.'

'Are you sure?'

'Yes.'

'How sure?'

'Very. It can hurt if you have the top of your ear pierced.'

'Why?'

'Because you've got small bones in your ear and it's more sensitive at the top.'

'You haven't got bones in your ear.'

'You have.'

'Haven't.'

'Have.'

'How do you know you have?'

'I just do.'

'My dad says that whenever I ask him how he knows stuff.'

'Well we did go to the same school.'

'I want my ear pierced when I'm older.'

'So do I,' agrees his brother before adding, 'and I want my nipple pierced as well.'

'That really hurts,' I point out.

'Why, have you got your nipple pierced?'

'No.'

'Well how do you know it hurts?'

'I just do.'

'See you said it again.'

'Sorry.'

'It's okay. Anyway how do you know it hurts?'

'Because.'

'Because what?'

'Because I know someone who had their nipple pierced and they stretched it and it bled when the needle was inserted.'

'Wow.'

'Wow,' says the other kid as well.

'Was it lots of blood?'

'I don't know, I wasn't there.'

'What did he do?'

'He went and had a few whiskeys.'

They both smile as if they understand and then one says his dad likes whiskey but he hasn't got his nipples pierced. I consider explaining that he requires the whiskey for a different type of pain, but they are too young to understand. Besides it's not answers that they seek but the opportunity for further questions.

They remain quiet for a short spell imagining and digesting all that they have learnt, their concentration occasionally lapsing with an odd push or kick to the other's legs. In their world a bruise on the shin is like a token of love, a sign of respect, recognition of the other's existence.

Soon one chirps up, 'I want my willy pierced when I'm older,' which is followed by the inevitable, 'Have you got your willy pierced?'

I sigh 'No' whilst imagining what it would be like, how much it would cost, and where I would get it done. I have no intention of drawing attention to my genitals just as I have no intention of drawing attention to my life.

'Does it hurt?'

'What?'

'Willy piercing.'

'I don't know.'

'Haven't you got any friends with their willy pierced?'

'No.'

They look rather disappointed at this, and I feel as if I have kind of let them down.

'Do you think it would hurt?'

'What do you think?'

'I don't know,' they giggle, but they do.

'Of course it bloody hurts.'

'Do you think people with their willy pierced drink whiskey?'

'Probably.'

A woman pushing a pram which looks more expensive than my car grimaces at our conversation. I can tell by the inoffensive floral patterns she has chosen to cover her child in, that penis mutilation is not her thing. I smile back towards her and tell the kids it's time to move on. Fortunately children are not ones to dwell and the conversation is forgotten when I mention a game of footy.

'But we've got no net.'

'We can make one.'

'Have I got to take my top off?'

'Not if you don't want to.'

'I don't want to', he smugly informs before adding, 'my dad always takes his off for us.'

Freezing for children is just one of the many tortures an adult must endure in a perverse logic which equates one person's suffering with another's joy.

They stare at me until I remove the clothing before giving each other a high five. They have no idea how to celebrate gracefully, but that's the beauty of being a child.

I shake my head, trying to remain motivated despite realising that I have lost this game before we have even started.

'What about the other post?'

'Are you going to have to take your t-shirt off?' enquires the other brother, as if this is the only thing that will do.

'No. We can use the sandwich bag.'

'But what if the sandwiches get crushed.'

'They won't.'

'How do you know they won't?'

'Because they won't.'

'What if they do?'

'Look, will you just stop moaning and worrying about things. You're like a couple of old women.'

Two women walking past stare across at me. They are not old but they are women, and so representative of the latter category. I want to chase after them and apologise by explaining the flaws of language and that I didn't mean what I said but something tells me this is an excuse they are already familiar with. Instead I decide to stick with the just as difficult task of trying to keep a couple of kids happy.

'Can we use one of your socks as a post instead?'

'NO. We use the sandwich bag or I'm taking you home.'

'You can't because our parents aren't back yet.'

'This is your last chance. Do you want to play football or not?'

They nod their heads and it seems to work. The minute you end the conversation with a dismissive unarguable point they accept it. I figure I must sound like their dad. Maybe when he's had a whiskey and just wants to rest.

'Where are we gonna make the goals?'

I look out at the masses of fields in front of me and wonder if they are taking the piss. They are not taking the piss they are waiting for an answer. I guess that's how it works in their house.

'Over there,' I say, pointing in the direction of a bin which has more rubbish around it than in it.

They ponder for a few seconds before pointing in the opposite direction. 'Can't we play over there instead?'

'No.'

'Why?'

'Because.'

'Because what?'

'Because I fucking said so.'

An old man walking his dog turns around and shakes his head.

'You swore,' says one kid.

'I know.'

'You're not meant to swear.'

'And you're not meant to question everything I say. Can't I just be the parent for once and you the child?'

'Okay,' they agree, as if I have finally made a reasonable request that doesn't seem to be too far fetched. 'Where are we playing?'

'Straight ahead.'

'What, near that couple?'

'Yes. Near that couple.'

'But the ball might hit them.'

'I know.'

'But they might get angry.'

'I know. I want to wake them from their calmed state.'

The kids laugh and walk ahead. Now that they know that I swear I'm not so bad.

'Do we get an extra goal if we hit them,' one eagerly enquires, whilst the more cautious of the two wants confirmation that if we do I will take all the blame. I decide not to reassure him until we have found the right spot.

The match starts and one of the kids takes a swipe at my ankle even though the ball is not around, manipulating situations to test the boundaries as only a child can. He's not laughing though when I leg him up, preventing an easy goal whilst sending him head first into some shit. He doesn't look too happy although his brother can't stop laughing.

'I wish your son was here.'

'So do I,' I point out.

'It would be two-a-side then and a bit more fairer. You're not very good on your own.'

'Can't you ring him?' asks the more resourceful brother.

'No.'

'Why?'

'Because he's with his mum.'

'Doesn't she like people ringing him? My mum doesn't mind my friends ringing me but I'm not allowed to ring them.'

'Look he's probably doing something with her.'

'Yeah, like shopping.'

'Does he like being with his mum?'

'I think so.'

'Do you think he prefers you or his mum?'

It is at this point that I release a thunderbolt that shoots into the imaginary top corner of the net and thuds against the back of some young lovers' heads.

The girl screams.

Her partner screams.

The kids scream.

I start to laugh.

I hate couples who spend the whole afternoon snogging in parks.

'Motherfucker,' shouts the girl, whose lip I think is bleeding although it may be the latest 'must have' colour in lipstick.

'You and your motherfucking kids.'

'They're not mine,' I retort.

'We're not his,' join in the kids, with what sounds more like relief than pride.

She gathers herself together, slightly ashamed at losing it in front of her partner and drags him to another part of the park.

'Do you think he's got his willy pierced?' asks one of the kids.

'I don't know, you better ask.'

'Have you got your willy pierced?' shouts one of the boys.

'And have you got your woman's willy pierced?' enquires the other.

But they are not listening. They stomp steadily away, probably more aware of the value of contraception now they have seen the truth about kids. Then they stop and start to kiss under a tree.

'Kids, have you heard of the African termite?'

One says yes and one says no.

'Well their life is worse than ours.'

'Because they haven't got Nintendo?'

'Partly, yes. Anyway they pass up and down tunnels all day on their way to the queen termite, whose job it is to give birth all the time until she dies.'

'Ur, that's disgusting.'

'Yeah, I'm glad that our Queen doesn't do that.'

'Me too, anyway, when they get to the queen termite they exchange saliva. She can tell by their saliva what kind of function they perform in the hive, and then knows what type of termite to give birth to next. This way the hive will always have the correct amount of workers, soldiers, etc.'

The kids seem disgusted.

'If I spat on the floor would a queen termite know what school I went to and what job I was going to get?'

'Maybe.'

'That's cool.' Then they both start to spit on the floor.

'Do termites have willies?'

'I don't know.'

'How come you know loads about spit and saliva and termites but you don't even know if they have willies?'

'I don't know.'

'What would happen if the queen termite was disabled?' but before I can respond to this question the other has had a revelation.

'Hey imagine if a Nottingham women gave birth to loads of ace footballers and they all played for Forest. That would be wicked.'

But his brother is more reasoned than his fellow sibling and points out, 'Man U would just buy them all.'

It is only when conversation starts and ends with football, taking love, kissing and African termites along its circuit, that the world does not seem so complicated but inextricably linked.

'I've got fizzy leg.'

'What's fizzy leg?' I enquire.

'It's when your leg gets fizzy.'

'You mean pins and needles?'

They both stare at me and start to laugh. I decide this conversation is not worth pursuing and try to tempt them from it with the lure of sandwiches.

'Are you ready for lunch?'

'Did the sandwiches get battered?'

'No, they didn't get battered.'

'What are they?'

'Veggie ham and tomato sauce.'

'But I'm not a vegetarian.'

'Well I am.'

'What's veggie ham anyway?'

'Its ham that's not made out of pigs.'

'So it's not ham then.'

'No.'

'Well why call it veggie ham then?' joins in the brother.

'Because it's for vegetarians and it's processed to look like ham.'

'But why would a vegetarian want to eat something that looked like ham? Why don't they just eat it if they like what it looks like?'

There is no point arguing with kids when they are right.

'Does it taste like ham?'

'Yes.'

'How can you be a vegetarian if you've tasted ham?'

'Because I wasn't always one.'

'Why change then?'

'Because I wanted to.'

'But why?'

'Because.'

'Because what?'

'Look I've been a vegetarian since I was about five.'

'How old are you?'

'Twenty-eight.'

'I know someone that's twenty-eight. My uncle Rob.'

'Do you want the veggie ham or not?'

'I suppose,' they both say.

'Is there anything else?'

'Crisps.'

'What sort?'

'Walkers.'

'Walkers what?'

'French Fries.'

'Cool, what flavour?'

'Worcester Sauce.'

'Ace.'

Once the food has been sanctioned I ask them where they want to sit. Both look around the park before shrugging their shoulders. As always I must make a decision of sorts.

'Do you mind if we sit on the bench near the ducks?'

'What ducks?' they ask.

'Those ducks,' I sigh.

'They're not ducks,' begins one, 'they're…'

'Geese,' finishes his brother.

I'm not 100% sure that they are correct but I don't care enough to argue.

Before the silver foil containing the sandwiches has been discarded the geese are upon us, making whatever noise it is that geese make. This makes the kids scream which in turn is mimicked by the geese in what could be described as a conversation of sorts. I can feel a headache coming on but soon the noise dies down. One of the kids has thrown the geese his crusts as a kind of peace offering.

I am tempted to tell them that this is the best part of the bread but

I'm not too sure that it is. It's just something I was told so many times as a child that I just accepted it as truth.

When I suggest giving the geese some French Fries crisps they look a little apprehensive. I figure that this is because they are their favourites and they don't want to share, but instead they reveal an uncharacteristic caring side to their personality.

'Will they choke on it?'

'No.'

'How do you know?'

'Because I've given them crisps before.'

'Were they French Fries?'

'No, Wotsits.'

The brothers both look at each other, and I can tell by the way they stop munching that there is nothing in the world as diverse as different brands of crisps. Fortunately I am spared a comparative analysis as a goose downs the French Fries in one, but not I might add without a wince and an erratic flapping of its wings. This makes them laugh and so they scatter the rest of the packet in the hope of seeing a repeat performance.

After much flapping, wincing and laughing I toss one a leftover chunk of my veggie ham sandwich. It is eagerly greeted and fought over, although only the bread is consumed and the ham spat out. Another less picky goose inspects the processed meat substitute before flying off.

The kids find this hilarious and their eyes sparkle as they explain, 'These geese are not vegetarian, they like proper ham.'

Although I feel a bit annoyed by the geese because I was under no obligation to share my food, I try to hide my anger. I don't know who the cheeky bastards think they are. But the kids won't let this go and so I endure ten minutes of insults which only ends when I hand them a Jaffa Cake.

'Can you get vegetarian Jaffa Cakes?'

'Shut it,' I tell them, wishing we had never stopped playing football.

The geese start to make their funny noises again and seem to be interested in the new food but the kids aren't as keen to share this time. One of them tells me that he asks his dad for Jaffa Cakes but he never gets them. The geese aren't put off though and have become accustomed to getting their own way over the years. One raises its wings above its head like a performing circus animal, but it has little chance with these Jaffa-deprived kids.

Eventually, and through perseverance rather than compassion, a goose is rewarded with a corner of a Jaffa Cake. I note that it is thrown at, rather than to the goose, and this must be their equivalent to kicking a ball at a young couple petting.

'Is there anything else?'

I look in the bag and pull out a cheese and onion roll which after one small bite they launch into the pond so that it sinks before the geese can eat it, obviously feeling bitter that they parted with their last chunk of Jaffa Cake. As they sit and curse the birds I wonder what it must be like to be a fish carefully swimming around, trying not to bump into other fish when from nowhere a cheese and onion roll comes floating down. It must be pretty surreal but more frightening is the realisation that the same could one day happen to me, that a massive cheese and onion roll could come flying out of space and hit me on the head. If this seems unlikely then put yourself momentarily in the position of the fish...

'Right it's time to go.'

'But we haven't spat on the fish yet?'

'What do you mean you haven't spat on the fish yet?'

They stare at me like I have just said the most stupid thing in the world.

'We just want to spit on them.'

'Only for a minute,' reasons the older brother.

'Does your dad know that you do that?'

'Yeah, but he pretends he can't see us. So, can we?'

'No you can't.'

'Why?'

'Must I quantify every single thing?'

'What does quantify mean?'

'It means you can't spit on the fucking fish, now come on we're going home.'

When I return the children their dad asks what they have been up to.

'We threw a cheese and onion roll at some fish and kicked a football at someone kissing and he swore.'

'Good, anything else?'

'No…Dad?'

'Yes.'

'I don't ever want to be a vegetarian…like him.'

'Well, you don't have to be.'

'Good.'

'Dad…'

'Yes.'

'Do you know anyone with their willy pierced?'

My friend looks at me but has known me long enough to know that there is no point asking. Instead he thanks me for looking after them and I tell him it's no problem.

The Three and a Half Day Parent

People say that having children hinders your life; this is not exactly true. What it does hinder is your drinking, which I suppose for some is pretty much the same thing. The hangovers become unbearable when the youngest is screaming which is why so many parents take up less physiological pursuits, like computer games, home decoration, and shopping for ingredients to make the latest Jamie Oliver recipe – all of which, unintentionally, encourage an early night's sleep. Fortunately I am a split-parent and so am spared such unimaginative forms of distraction. For three and a half days I have my son and 'do stuff' and for the other three and a half days I 'do drink'. I find this contrast serves my needs well.

We, the 'ex' and I, agreed upon equal access which is a little bit more than we agreed upon whilst together. Neither of us wanted the indignity of being a weekend parent. We considered using our child as a means of emotionally blackmailing the other but decided against it as it took up too much energy. He'll probably hold it against us when he's older given that parental squabbling is the common experience of most of his friends, but I'm sure he'll get over it. The beauty of this system is he is cherished by whichever parent he is with, and compensation for the other comes in the form of added free time, often spent in the company of the local barman.

To some extent I would say that split-parenting is the way forward. It works for me in a way that marriage didn't. Besides, nobody I know has ever remained married and so perhaps future generations should start with split-parenting the minute their child is born. This may seem negative, but then that which is closest to 'truth' often is. Take an incident that happened this morning. I was in a good mood because it was my day to pick him up from school and so in my last few hours of solitude I decided to travel into town. Directly in front of me on the bus were a small kid and his mum. The kid was remarkably well dressed and so I thought I would commend him on his appearance.

'You look very smart, been to a job interview?'

'I'm too young to work.'

'I feel the same way, and I'm old enough.'

'I know,' the boy replied before he added, 'but you don't work anyway.'

'How do you know?' I asked

'I've seen ya pick ya kid up from school. He's in my mate's class.'

I don't think he was having a pop, I think it was more of a social observation. Keen to distract him from my employment history I continued my investigation into his smart attire to which he curtly replied, 'I've bin ta court ta stop me dad from seeing me.'

At this point his mother decided to join in the conversation by placing her hand firmly on his leg, just above where the kneecap bends, a reward perhaps for what she probably classed as loyalty. She had a large hand and thin fingers, combined I imagine they made a useful team, adaptable and able to get to grips with any situation.

I just looked at the kid and smiled. Sometimes that's all you can do. I considered pulling at his ear or ruffling his hair but decided against it. I figured if I made any move in his direction his mother's hand would spring from his leg and pull me down to the ground. I didn't need that and he didn't need that, besides this may be the most affection he has had all week. It's weird how a kid so young can behave so old.

I decided to break the silence again. There's something wrong when a child just sits quiet on a bus looking straight ahead without any inclination for distraction.

'Do you like football?'

'My dad does.'

'Who does he support?'

'I don't know.'

'Do you play football?'

'Sometimes.'

'I bet you'll be glad to get out those clothes when you get home and put on some…'

It was at this point his mother interrupted.

'Why are you so fucking obsessed with his clothes? Are you a pervert or something?'

'I was just…'

'Don't fucking anything.'

As she spoke I could see her knuckles whitening where they were gripping her child's leg. I decided to get off the bus a few stops early, figuring the walk and the fresh air would do me some good. As the bus drove off the woman gave me the finger, whilst her son continued to stare off into the distance.

I am glad that my former wife and I had managed to resolve things amicably, that our son didn't have to put on matching shirt and trousers and inform strangers on buses that he had been to court to stop his dad from seeing him. I liked our arrangement: three and a half days of drinking and then three and a half of Nintendo, walks, football, *Shrek*, *Crazy Bones*, *Pokemon* and all the rest. The knowledge that I will always be able to pick him up at the same time on the same day each week enables me to get through the week as a Friday night once had. It is a very simple arrangement that most find hard to agree on.

I guess because of this I feel like the luckiest man alive, like I have been given a second chance and I wish other parents would allow themselves to feel the same as well, to gain from splitting up rather than putting each other through unnecessary pain. Take tonight for instance. My son and I drove to Coventry to see stock car racing because he likes to hear bangs and loud noise. If it wasn't for split-parenting I would probably be slumped in front of the TV, content to embroil myself in the narrative of fictional characters rather than create a story of my own. I'd never have had the energy or inclination to discover this 'place' and its magical sect. This gloriously vile smelly pit where cars snarl and their owners roar and the food bars fail to cater for vegetarians. The mechanical madness offers a temporary reprieve from the monotony of human conversation whilst the exhaust fumes itch at the eyes as if punishment for witnessing the earlier misery of other people's lives. I'd never have discovered such places if it had not been for the constant need to entertain my son.

I would not have discovered the stock car racing circuit either if I were a non-parent because my friends would have immediately taken the piss on any suggestion to come here. If I was still married then neither of us would have been bothered because routine wears you down. It beats you into a pulp where pennies are constantly counted and freedom can only be found in an hour's soak in the bath. It is for this reason I believe split-parenting is the way forward. It allows a balancing of needs as well as expanding horizons and, perhaps most importantly, an awareness of the fragility of time.

When we got home that evening I tucked him up in bed and kissed him on the line of freckles that sometimes get hidden beneath his hairline. One day he'll be a good looker, just like his mum.

'What football team do I support?'

'Why are you asking me a stupid question for?'

'Because sometimes dads need a stupid answer. Now what team do I support?'

He looks at me and mumbles under his breath, 'Derby'.

'What did you say?' I ask in mock horror, whilst adjusting my fingers in preparation for a tickle.

'Forest,' he laughs, 'you support Forest, and so do I.'

Hamadryas Baboons and Lisa Lashes

I took my son to Windsor Safari Park once. A baboon climbed onto the bonnet of my car and just sat there supinely, as if it was its rightful place. My son laughed whilst the baboon looked upwards, unaware. I lit a cigarette and my son started to cough so I extinguished it. It was a clear stakeout and I had all the time in the world, although it looked as if the *Papio hamadryas* was in no rush either. Given that the average life span of a baboon in captivity is around thirty-seven years it could potentially be a long wait. I figured now was a good time to think of a more plausible reason for returning our son at potentially forty-five years old, rather than the following morning as originally agreed.

My son asked me what the baboon was doing and I told him: 'sitting on my bonnet'. He wasn't happy with the answer and asked why he was sitting on the bonnet. I explained I didn't know and that it was feasible it was simply a primate bred to sit. He didn't seem too impressed with that either so I explained about its ischial callosities, or leathery sitting pads, which allow the baboon to not only sit, but sleep upright as well. My son seemed sceptical of my parental omnipotence and so I applied simple logic, explaining that the average baboon weighed between 14 and 40kg and therefore was glad to rest its muscular frame. Typically he asked: if this was the case then why didn't elephants sit down more often, before smugly looking upwards. Taking a momentary pause I explained that if elephants sat down they probably wouldn't be able to get back up again. Returning his smug look it was finally my chance to look upwards, but he turned away. Probably trying to find another way to catch his father out, given as this was his favourite pastime.

During this discussion the baboon had reclined onto my windscreen as if enjoying a rare British sun. Either that or it was trying to listen in on our conversation. I think the baboon had less to do in its life than I, and in a perverse way that made me feel slightly better. As it closed its eyes I considered switching on my windscreen wipers but I figured this would only serve as a fan and would hardly move it. Besides, it wasn't every day you got to make eye contact with a *Papio hamadryas* and so was worth the study. I was struck by its dog-like muzzle; you could see why they didn't need knives and forks. It reminded me of the long slender barrel of a gun and I felt slightly relieved that if it fired, its bullets would only be seeds, roots and insects, as for a primate it had a pretty unadventurous diet.

'Dad he's still there.'

'I know son. Everyone knows. Maybe that's why he's doing it.'

'What do you mean?'

'I mean, perhaps he is showing off. Or maybe he likes the feel of cars. Stuck up in the trees with all those cutting branches and enveloping leaves of green must get pretty depressing. Maybe he's bored of all that nature shit and wants a nice smoothly finished bonnet to perch his smoothly finished rump on for a change. Sound reasonable to you?'

'I suppose so,' he replied.

'Well now you know a bit more about baboons son.' I felt proud that I had performed my parental duties by handing down some irrelevant knowledge I could convince him would be useful in future years. The day was turning out to be a success.

'Can we see the lions? I've seen enough of the baboon. I'm glad my bum isn't red.'

'Maybe he's not glad his bum is red and that's why he's sticking it in our faces. So we can feel his pain. He may be a protester baboon.'

'I didn't know there was such thing as protester baboons.'

'Well you do now son.'

I revved the engine a bit to indicate that it was time to move but it merely rocked the baboon to a comforting sleep. I wondered what it was dreaming about and if it had nightmares, did they involve its principle enemy, the leopard, or did such fears come symbolically disguised like our own?

'Please move?' I politely requested, taking greater care with tone of voice than with content of words.

'He's a stubborn bastard.'

'You swore.'

'I'm sorry.'

'It's alright. Mum swears as well.' I was glad our bad habits were equilateral.

'How do you know it's a he?'

'Because females grow to roughly twenty-five pounds which is half the weight of the male. Besides he has a silver-grey mane running from his shoulders which means he is a mature male. Hey, that means he could be around thirty, which means we might get out of here before you're fifteen.'

My son scratched his nose, warning me of imminent confusion. Perhaps he had forgotten that baboons' average age of death was thirty-seven and hence the long wait to get him off the car, but it was something more specific that was working in his head.

'Dad, don't you ever get fat female baboons?'

I didn't really want to get into this one and so I lit a cigarette. He knew that always meant I was relaxing and didn't want to be disturbed. Instead he coughed again, which was his way of conveying he enjoyed breathing, and so once more I extinguished the cigarette. You literally give up everything for your kids. I decided to hedge my frustration back at the baboon.

'Come on there's other cars too,' I reasoned, but he wasn't listening. He obviously had a penchant for the Nissan Primera.

I started to laugh.

'Why are you laughing dad?'

'Because there's a baboon on my car and he won't get off.'

'Maybe he doesn't want to get off like you said.'

'Maybe.'

I decided to put on a little music and selected hard house over chill-out. I pumped up the volume and my son started to laugh and the baboon made a funny noise and then another baboon came and sat on my bonnet. I started to become a little worried now as I knew baboons generally travelled in groups of sixty and these groups usually made up a troop of around 200. Fortunately rationale kicked in and I realised that there were probably about ten *Papio hamadryas* in the safari. They could probably just about all fit on.

I took the Lashes tape out of the slot, as I didn't want to encourage further conviviality especially as the tempo had quickened and was about to peak with the track *Luckin' Good*. I replaced it with the chill-out one instead, something less evocative. Instantly the other baboon got off, smearing its arse across the windscreen before scurrying off on all fours.

'I guess we can confirm that as a general rule, baboons prefer Lisa Lashes.'

My son did not look any more enlightened by the fact and seemed more preoccupied with whether the lions would like Lisa Lashes and so I gently started to move forward.

Now I never meant to kill the baboon, I swear. But he just wouldn't get down and we had gone past the stage of rational negotiation. I simply revved my engine and shook him about, but nothing happened. Its only function was to bob its arse up and down in front of my eyes like a hypnotic yo-yo. I thought of Camus in *The Outsider* and how the sun had got to him, leading to murder. You can get used to anything in life. This baboon had clearly had enough of baboon life. It was sick of all the grooming that socially united the group. Picking nits and fleas out of each other's hair was not relaxing and uniting as anthropologists had claimed, but boring! The lack of want was another casuistic misconception. It was sick of the pressure that came with being the dominant gender. It wasn't such a utopia having exclusive breeding rights to females and being able to monitor and control their every move. He just wanted to lie in the sun, on my bonnet, and this car was his ticket out of here.

Perhaps I should have given him the keys and traded places? I don't think anybody would have noticed and as long as my son was returned home on time it wouldn't bother his mother. Besides our cultures are synonymous; large dominant males rule the troops and are responsible for diffusing fractious members and protecting the colony from predators. By our system, size is replaced with suits.

I wasn't going that fast, probably averaging twenty-five mph, just enough to send a small breeze blowing into the baboon's face. I must admit he did look pretty cool and the females seemed impressed. It put equivalent mating rituals to shame. Suddenly my son shouted out, 'Dad it's the lions, put on your Lisa Lashes tape.' The baboon must've heard because it jumped off the bonnet and got its tail caught in the grill. By the time I had braked it had already been decapitated.

My son started to cry and I started to smoke and this time he didn't cough. I tried to explain to him that it was fate; that some species of baboon had evolved a stump rather than a tail and it was just the way things are. This did not placate him and I wondered which story his mother would prefer if she had a choice? That I didn't return him until he was forty-five because I had to wait for a baboon to die or that he had witnessed his father decapitate a *Papio hamadryas?* As with this particularly unlucky species of baboon, I couldn't win. So I drove off from the scene of the crime and hoped the lions would take their role in the evolutionary ladder and dispose of the evidence.

On my return to civilised society I was greeted by my own evolutionary king predator; the police. They shook their heads from side to side and felt the need to lecture me before my arrest, extracting morality at any given opportunity as if it was some preordained right.

They told me that they personally detested cowards like me who fled from the scene of the crime instead of facing up to my responsibilities. They told me there were witnesses and I didn't know if they were referring to the elephants or the giraffes or the car behind. It really had been one of those days and I just wish I had changed places. I could be surrounded by sixty friends all grooming my hair and offering up sex now.

In court the moral sermon left the judge flustered. He squeezed every last drop of air out of his body as if keeping it would contaminate him in some way. It left his face red and for one small moment all I could see was the baboon's arse. Then he showed a photograph of the decapitated animal to the jury. They sighed, and for a brisk moment it sounded comforting, like a wave crashing against sand. For such cruelty I was banned for life from zoos, and pet shops, and sentenced to a month's hard labour. He did not believe in the concept of accident, a sentiment applauded by the jury. As they led me away I realised I had served twenty-eight years on this planet and never paid my council tax late, never had a fight or tried to spin my gas meter the opposite way around. I kill one baboon that's off his tree and I am a criminal.

Never Marry a Therapist or Have More Kids than Fingers

There is nothing I love more than visiting my friend when I have a hangover because whenever I see his life, mine feels instantaneously better. He is married to a therapist and has more kids than I have fingers. Whenever I see him he pulls me to one side and gives me advice, 'Never marry a therapist, you can't do anything.' Other times he will pull me to one side and say, 'Never have loads of kids, you can't do anything.' Whenever he passes on advice he is usually right, although I cannot understand why he insists on living the life he warns me about. I don't think he understands either, maybe his wife does.

My girlfriend and I equally enjoy observing his torture. We derive most pleasure from the knowledge that we can leave and he must stay. It gives us a sense of freedom that we perhaps otherwise would not appreciate. We always smile as we wave goodbye and my girlfriend insists on shutting his gate. Perhaps making sure that he and his children and therapist wife can't escape.

My friend has started to scratch his back and head a lot. It is not a nervous reaction but more of a compulsive disorder. When he does it his wife shouts at him to stop. She explains that he is repressing his anger and that he should go to the 'angry corner' at the back of the garden if he has anything he needs to let out. She tells him that his behaviour is dysfunctional and that the children need a role model, an adult, not another child. He apologises and asks if he can go outside to shout in the angry corner.

Once I heard him shouting in the angry corner. His head was directed at the ground and he was quite clearly taking his frustration out on a worm that had temporarily surfaced. He shouted lots of things and there was more on his mind than he ever let on to me. It serves no purpose to reiterate his angst but you got the impression that maybe he was still a child, as only a child could have the imagination to juxtapose the words he was using.

When he left the angry corner I knelt down and took a good look at the worm. I wondered if it had ears and if so what must it be thinking now. It's probably riddled with guilt after hearing that confessional and grateful for the simplicity of its existence. It must be a pretty blissful life to squirm in and out of mud all day. Just twisting and turning in darkness. As I tried to figure out the lifestyle of this strange parasite one of his kids came over. He told me that his mum had sent him, that I wasn't allowed to just stand in the angry corner and do nothing. If I wanted to do that I should go to church and pray, even though there was no such thing as God. He told me that his mum thought religion was like cheap therapy and that it infringed upon her business. He then told me they had a thoughtful corner in the shed and if I didn't feel like shouting I could go and sit in there. I asked him if he ever went in there but he said he didn't because it was boring. He then started to shout.

'What are you doing?'

'Getting angry.'

'Why?'

'Cause it's the angry corner.'

He was soon joined by two brothers and a sister. I think it was their sister although I can't recollect seeing her before. They all started to shout and I began to think, perhaps this is why the worm comes up for air. He hears the shouting and has to inspect. It's just like fish when it rains and they come to the surface thinking there is food. I pointed out the worm to the kids although I had to shout 'there's a worm' as they couldn't hear me above the noise.

One of the kids took a half-broken cricket stump that lay against the fence and pierced it through the worm, splitting it in two.

'What are you doing?' I asked, 'No don't tell me, it's the angry corner, so you're killing the worm.'

'No I'm not. Worms can rejoin together.'

'Have you ever seen them do it?'

'No.'

'How do you know then?'

He paused and then with all the confidence of a ministerial press agent, declared 'Mum told me.'

I went back into the house and my friend was still scratching. He was making ten cups of tea in cups with missing handles. It's a pity cups couldn't re-animate themselves; he obviously couldn't afford any new ones. I asked my friend why he never boiled the kettle when he made tea and he told me the kettle was broken. He then began to explain that it was inconsequential. By the time he had made all the drinks and found the relevant child or adult they were cold anyway. He began to scratch some more, using the tip of his nail so as to gradually break through the surface of the skin.

He never used to scratch so purposefully, as if he was actually trying to shed skin like a snake. But despite his efforts it won't come off, reminding him once more of his ineffectuality. I think he knows this though and so there is no point me telling him. Instead I try to ignore him when he does it by fixating on bits of torn wallpaper.

Once my girlfriend went up and scratched his back for him. He looked guiltily at me and said, 'We're not having an affair.' I told him I knew they weren't and he looked relieved, like I was the first person in the world who had digested what he had said.

I like his kids the most. They are eternally dirty and I have come to suspect they wash in mud. They are always dismantling something or blatantly destroying it. This applies to anything within their range. A neighbour's cat, a fence, a sycamore tree, an old washing machine, toys, dining room table, hi-fi, cupboards, anything and everything they can get their hands on. Sometimes they break things they have already broken. At Christmas instead of unwrapping presents they jump on them or try to set them on fire, or drop them out of windows to unwrap the packaging. 'Leave them, it's best the anger is out than in,' informs his wife, as my friend starts scratching.

One year I bought them all a present, which I smashed before wrapping it up. When they opened the presents they just stared at me like I was a fool. 'It's broke mister,' said one. 'You owe us a new one,' said another. After a few hours one of them asked me if it could be fixed and with a little bit of glue I made the necessary repair. On seeing this, the other kids followed by example and after four hours I had rebuilt all the present. All the kids jumped on me at once and said it was the best presents they had ever had. It made me feel a little sad. Then they jumped on them and smashed them into a thousand pieces and threw them in the garden with the rest.

My friend tells me that he has to get angry more. I ask him why, and he goes all shy. His wife walks into the room and shouts at him for not defending himself. He tells me that he has issues and ambitions and he is going to start putting his dreams into action. I don't actually think he knows what he is saying but I go along with him because he is married to a therapist and he doesn't need shit from me as well. He tells me that you have to be positive in life. That it doesn't matter what happens to you it's how you deal with it that matters. Later when I am drinking a cup of tea he asks me if it is half full or half empty. I just look at him and say 'cold'.

My friend's wife is constantly rediscovering herself through expensive self-help books and philosophy which rather than bringing enlightenment often bring confusion. This is because she reads so many books without pausing so that none have time to settle and grow. This week his wife is reading a book about reincarnation. She wants to get in touch with her previous lives. She believes that she was a soldier in 1485 and was responsible for the battle of Bosworth. I tell her that's a big burden to carry on her shoulders and she informs me it wouldn't be so big if her husband lent her some support. I figure he can't whilst he is making dinner for more children than I have fingers, but allow her to continue. She tells me that in a past life my friend caused a blockage in heaven so great that the new souls couldn't be born as the old souls passed through. She told me if I was having problems grasping the seriousness of this then I should imagine the current railway system and multiply it by ten. Then she pointed a finger at my mate. 'Him,' she said, and shook her head, as he began to scratch his arm.

My friend thought he had a pretty easy ride when she was reading books on quantum physics as he was able to deny that he was actually ever there each time she accused him of doing something wrong. But his wife was quick to point out that as this life would then be subjected to infinite variables he was accountable for every single thing that had gone wrong with the world.

It was quite quiet in his house when his wife went through her nihilist stage. Every time he asked her something she refused to answer because there was no point. Similarly there was no point in pointing out all his bad points as what's the point if we are going to die anyway? His scratching ceased for a while. Not because he was no longer a nervous wreck but because he had read one of her books and realised there was no point to scratching either.

My girlfriend's favourite stage was the Feng Shui. When his wife had determined which window was the most calming the children were only allowed to smash up toys at the opposite end of the house. This meant, for a couple of weeks at least, you were guaranteed a temporary reprieve. No child was likely to come and crush a Power Ranger over your skull.

My girlfriend and I would always want to leave the house at roughly the same time. We had a similar threshold and the wisdom to know when enough was enough. It may have been too many cold teas or having too many items from your bag broken by the kids. Or perhaps it was the two-hour conversation with his wife about self-realisation, who knows? But something would click and we would have to go. We would be around next month on the last Sunday.

As we reversed out the drive all the kids would shout goodbye, some would throw Lego at the bonnet, whilst another would opt for a water gun filled with paint. My mate ran up to the window as he would every time we left after a visit.

'You are gonna come back aren't you?'

'Of course.'

'Promise.'

'I promise.'

Then he would take my girlfriend's hand and ask her if she had any desires to become a therapist and she would smile and say 'fuck off'. He would then look at me, telling me I had a good one there, and I didn't want to gloat so I just smiled back.

I don't know why but when we got back we used to have the best sex ever and then we would sit silent for hours, breathing into each other and occasionally planting kisses on whatever the nearest part of the body to our mouths was; communication, without the hindrance of words.

The White Van Man

The kids put their jackets or jumpers at the end of the street to make imaginary goalposts. They laugh and shout, occasionally tripping over and cutting a knee. Sometimes they push, sometimes they pull, and occasionally a bit of both. It is all the boys from odd-numbered houses against all the boys from even-numbered houses, but in their heads it is Forest versus Derby. Sometimes sisters are allowed to join in but they soon stop playing because nobody will pass the ball. It is the kind of attitude they have come to expect from all boys, whether from the odd- or even-numbered houses on the street.

An occasional ball lands in a garden and they momentarily pause. A system is developed where they take it in turns to retrieve the ball. They are in and out, with heads bowed low to avoid the occupant who will castigate them for crushing some flowers or for not shutting the gate. Sometimes it lands in number forty-three where instead of retrieving a pig's bladder you would think some kind of political negotiation was going on. I suppose learning tolerance is not such a bad quality to install into the young. To avoid conflict I have seen them use fishing nets, skipping ropes, and any other instrument that may release the ball from the clutches of overgrown lawns. But generally speaking the neighbours are accommodating, because one of their kids is involved in the game.

Then the white van man screeches into the street, runs over the kids' clothes, tramples the goalposts, and parks his mechanical horse in the middle of the pitch. It is something that never happens to those players who grace the City Ground, and puts an end to their imaginary match as it does at the same time every night.

The van driver jumps down from his white horse and fills the air with immediate rhetoric, a football supporter in his own right.

'Go and play somewhere else.'

'Don't moan if you get run over. You shouldn't be playing on the streets.'

'If your clothes are ruined don't bother telling your mum it was me. A road is for driving over and that includes anything in the way.'

The kids tug at their crumpled clothing, place the ball under their arms and return to their homes sad, now the ultimate referee has blown a close to their game. They shuffle off to their respective sides of the street and a unanimous decision is made as to who won the game, then it is challenges and banter in preparation for the inevitable rematch.

When the kids are gone and there is no one to shout at, the white van man looks sad. He has been locked up for too long in his van and he is desperate for human company but in his eagerness to communicate he only frightens people away. It is a lonely existence and the only warmth he has comes from the parcels he faithfully delivers. I watch him lock up and he watches me, watching him. He tells me in no uncertain terms what he will do to the kids if the ball hits his van. He tells me what he will do to the kids if they trample his flowers. There is no point telling him there are no flowers in his garden and that the kids have now gone. He does not need to listen. He needs to talk. When he gets home, he will need to eat. Then he will need to sleep. He may need to fuck at some point, but it is not as regular as the other essentials that dominate his world.

The next day the kids play football. It is 3-2. It is Forest versus Barnsley and strangely is more interesting than if you were actually watching Forest versus Barnsley. One girl's persistence pays off and she is allowed to go in goal; a diet based on cola cubes and Mr Kipling cakes has sculptured a frame large enough to fill the entire net. The white van zooms around the corner. You can hear his exhaust blowing up the street. The kids are in a mass scramble fighting for possession of the ball. They stop playing just as his van screeches around the corner. An instinct that keeps them there right to the last second, sucking every moment of freedom they can and then they scarper back to their homes. Praising each other on a certain goal or move during the game and then discussing what 'Marlon Harewood would have done'. Although one jokes that he would probably have run into the van.

They have accepted the rules as only children can learn to do. Kids can deal with anything once it becomes a part of everyday. It is a silly world with silly rules that cramps their enjoyment and freedom, but one which they dutifully respect. It is good that it doesn't wear them down now as it will in later years. I however am worn down and instead of a near miss I can only see the potential of death.

'You could have killed one of them,' I point out.

'Good,' he shouts back before adding, 'there's nothing stopping them playing up the park.'

I hear one kid mumble to another that they are not allowed to play up the park because there are dirty syringes. I don't think any of them know this for certain, rather it is something they have heard their parents say; a convenient morality given that to play up there would entail a lift.

The white van man senses this. He points to his dirty van and explains, 'This is proper dirt' and how it can only be obtained from a hard days graft. Emblazoned in the dirt is the notorious graffiti of 'also available in white' written on both sides. It seems to be on all the vans in this area and I wonder if it is a Nottingham thing, the kind of obvious humour that appears to obvious-minded men. He points to a mark on his van and declares it's a ball mark. I tell him it's a branch mark. He asks me what the fuck do I know, so I think what the hell, and tell him.

'Firstly the mark you are pointing to is not rotund, which is the shape you would expect a spherical object to make. Secondly, your van is scratched and has red marks, which indicates to me you have been snared by a hawthorn tree which is thorny, covered in berries and most commonly found in hedgerows. Can you remember passing a group of twelve-metre-high trees with bright brown flaky bark?'

He bellows, 'You *Guardian*-reading…clunt,' and then whilst staring at my clean red car adds, 'What the fuck do you know about anything?'

I do not have time to answer such an open-ended question and instead shrug my shoulders as he tells me what he knows; which is, kids should be in bed. They should be seen and not heard and that parents don't beat their kids enough. He then tells me about how he has to drive to Sheffield every day, which obviously annoys him to the extent that he cannot even resist telling me his preferred route. He then pats his van, shakes his head and shouts something about not needing any shit from liberals and unruly brats after a hard day's work.

I feel sorry for the kids on our street; everybody wants to blame them for something. I sometimes think the neighbours were born thirty-six and have forgotten what it was like to be young. Is it not enough that their fantasies and role playing involve becoming Nottingham Forest?

I am girded into action as someone has to defend these kids and so I creep out of bed at some post-midnight hour. I walk up to his van and on close inspection am delighted to find I was right about the marks being from the hawthorn tree and I can tell by the jagged shape made by the leaves. Instead I write 'National Front Rules', safe in the knowledge that he will probably receive a good kicking when up in Sheffield when he tries to run over Sheffield kids playing football in the streets. He will be incriminated as a racist rather than the lesser label of careless driver, which always allows him to get off.

No sooner have I vented my spleen I find myself rubbing it off. This is not my world and it's not how I operate. If he receives a black eye it will only end up as a black eye for someone else. This system operates too frequently in life and is why nothing ever gets sorted out. Instead I go back to my house and return with a bucket full of soapy suds and I clean his van. When it has been cleaned I give it a polish with some Turtle Wax I never had the energy to use on my own car. I am tempted to write 'also available in grey' but figure this would ruin the gesture. It takes me three hours but feels longer as I am aware he is snoring in bed and probably farting on his wife's leg as he sleeps.

When he awakes he looks confused. He walks around his van inspecting it. He can see his face reflected off the bonnet and it looks like Dorian Gray. He twists his head around, hoping to find the culprit peeking out from behind a bush. When he can find nobody he drives off.

That evening as the kids play football, it is Forest versus Coventry and it's the FA Cup third round. The score is 4-4 and it's one of the best games I have seen all week. The girl who used to play in goal is having a blinder up front. Suddenly the distant noise of a spluttering van can be heard gaining momentum. The girl is through with a shooting opportunity but at the last minute picks up the ball; not prepared to get run over for a win, she valiantly decides upon a draw.

As the kids walk away, the white van man tries to reverse over one but they are wise to his antics and dodge his attempted tackle. He shouts at them, telling them they should be in bed. He warns that a ball had better not hit his fence and then threatens to buy a dog that will rip their ball to shreds. I smile and wave at him and he tells me it's about time I got a job, as he slams shut his rusty gates to keep the rest of the world out.

That night his van only takes an hour to clean and I don't even have to polish it because it still has its sheen. As I have saved so much time I decide to apply some *Hammerite* to his gate and give it a little oil as well. I sleep in the next morning and so miss out on his reaction but I don't mind. Now the gate shimmers in the sunlight, it looks quite beautiful.

His van makes a different noise to usual when we hear it coming up the road. Perhaps an annual MOT has given it the extra bit of bite it had been missing before. The kids are in the middle of a boring 0-0 draw and to my great disappointment are starting to play more and more like Forest each day. As he veers into the street he drives closer to the children than he has done all year. He seems intent on popping the ball but the worrying thing is the ball is in the arms of one of the boys. It is a lucky escape and I think the only reason he didn't kill the child is he would no longer have someone to shout at.

He exits his van and with it the usual rhetoric exits his mouth. The kids continue walking as if nothing has happened. He slams shut his gate and he slams shut his front door and he will no doubt slam down his food and maybe on to his wife as well.

That night I clean his van and pay particular attention to the grill. It is full of dead insects he has unknowingly killed. Perhaps I should have left them as it would probably cheer him up to know he has had such a profound effect on the world. I plant a few flowers around his garden path and have been careful not to select any with thorns so as not to wind him up. I even find time to give his lawn a little trim which takes me a good four hours as I have to do it all by hand so as not to wake him. By the time I have finished it is only 4.45 a.m. so I varnish his door and porch to stop it rotting in the rain. I even place a little bench I no longer use in the middle of his grass, just so he has the option of sitting when he shouts at the kids.

The next night, he comes home earlier than usual. He is not driving as fast and the kids do not run when he pulls up. They know something has changed to their schedule and they wait to find out what it is, what new rule they must adhere to if they are to share the same space. Instead of jumping out and slamming his door he sort of clambers out. He looks at the kids and instead of shouting at them he just stares. The children stare back and one with his front teeth missing smiles. The white van man goes mad. Perhaps he has false teeth and thinks the young lad is taking the piss.

He screams that he doesn't like flowers because they give him hay-fever and that the smell of wood varnish gives him a headache. He screams that he likes his lawn overgrown because then he can't see children out his window. He complains that his gate was not sanded down before it was painted and the bench is so damp if he sits on it he'll get piles. He explains that his van is his job and people shouldn't clean it because if they caused any damage he would get the blame. Were they trying to get him the sack when all he wants to do is earn some money?

He then muttered something about painting your own houses and leaving him in peace and about how he was going to buy a dog that would rip apart their ball and tear it to shreds. Then he slammed his door shut so hard it rattled the window pane, but thankfully it did not break. The kids turned around and went back home and I opened up the pages of *The Guardian*, realising that perhaps not everybody in the world wants your help.

Author Biographies

David Bateman is a poet and story-writer living in Liverpool. His solo poetry publications include *Curse Of The Killer Hedge* (Iron 1996), and *A Homage To Me* (Driftwood 2003). Two further collections, *More Spit Than Polish*, and *The Sweetness Of Nightingales*, are forthcoming from Driftwood.

Boyan Biolchev was born in Sofia in 1942. He has been Head of the Department of Slavonic Literatures since 1992. From 1991 until 1999, he was Dean of the Faculty of Slavonic Philology and in 1999 he was elected Rector of the University of Sofia.

Boyan's work, short stories and novels, have been translated and published across Europe. He has written the scripts of six Bulgarian feature films and a twelve-episode television program co-produced by Bulgarian National Television and RAI, Italy, which has been distributed in 136 countries. He publishes his short stories regularly in the Bulgarian press.

Andrew Clancy is Irish, but was lured away from the rain by the charms of a French lady. Now living in Paris, he is completing work on a short story collection and a novel. This is his first published work.

Diane Cockburn holds an MA in Creative Writing from Northumbria University and teaches creative writing in Durham. Her work has been published in a range of anthologies, including *Discoverers* edited by Chrissie Glazebrook (Mudfog Press).

Svetlana Dicheva was born in 1960 in Plovdiv, Bulgaria. She is a leading journalist on Bulgarian National Radio and Television, specializing in the sphere of cultural journalism. Her first fiction book, *The Balkan Prophet*, was published in 2000.

Crista Ermiya is of Filipino and Turkish-Cypriot parentage, grew up in London and now lives in Newcastle-upon-Tyne. Her short fiction has appeared on Pulp.net and in the anthologies *Wonderwall* (Route), *Parenthesis* (Comma Press), and *Tell Tales III*.

Zdravka Evtimova was born in 1959. In Bulgaria she has published four collections of short stories and three novels: *Your Shadow was My Home*, *Lindy* and *Thursday*. Her novel *God of Traitors* was published in June 2004 as an E-book by Buck Publications, Dallas, Texas, USA. Her short story collection *Bitter Sky* was published by Skrev Press in 2003. Zdravka has won a number of literary prizes including the Gencho Stoev literary award of Balkani Publishers for a short story written by a Balkan author in March 2004. Her novel *Thursday* won the Prose Award of the Bulgarian Writers' Union for 2003. Zdravka works as a literary translator and at present she is working on her PhD thesis on Toni Morrison's novels. She lives with her husband, two sons and her daughter in Pernik, Bulgaria.

Carla Gericke was born in South Africa and moved to the United States in 1995. She practised law in both countries before turning to writing full time. Her work has appeared in literary journals, anthologies and online. Carla lives with her husband in New York. 'When We Talk About Words' won the Irwin and Alicia Stark Award for outstanding short fiction.

Kathleen Jones has published journalism, short fiction, and eleven books – nine non-fiction titles (including biographies of Christina

Rossetti and Catherine Cookson) and two poetry collections. She is currently working on a biography of Katherine Mansfield, and is an on-line creative writing tutor for the Open University. She lives in Cumbria.

James Lawless was born in Dublin and lives in Kildare. He is an arts graduate of UCD and has an MA from DCU. He has had stories and poems broadcast on radio and published in newspapers, journals and anthologies in Ireland and England. He won the Scintilla Welsh Open Poetry competition in 2002 and the Cecil Day Lewis play section award in 2005 for a play entitled, *What Are Neighbours For?*

Katherine Locke was Reader in Residence for the BBCs Big Read and has worked with various community groups on literature development projects. She is currently employed as Reader in Residence for children in care in Dorset. The aim of the post is to promote reading for pleasure opportunities for children in foster care and the children's homes in the county. Katherine is also a reader for the Bridport Prize. She lives in Dorset with her partner, two children and four stepchildren.

Rochita Loenen-Ruiz is originally from the Philippines and now lives in the Netherlands with her husband and family. 'My Skin, Us' is part of a poetic memoir that she is working on, entitled *Letters to the Other.*

Daithidh MacEochaidh, writer and founder of Skrev Press, lives and works in Hebden Bridge with partner Nicky and their two children: Abby and Ursula Niamh.

Katy Massey is a college lecturer, freelance journalist, writer and poet. She is working on a creative non-fiction memoir, of which 'Morphea' forms a part, and is currently undertaking research for a PhD at Newcastle University.

Benjamin Mellor is from Hertfordshire and has lived in Manchester since 2000. He is a freelance writer and theatre practitioner, performs regularly at spoken word events and is currently developing a solo show as part of an *At Home* artist residency at Contact theatre.

Nicky O'Neill is a Creative Writing lecturer at the Open University. She has published two novels and a collection of short stories under the name of Harlow. She lives in Hebden Bridge with her partner and two daughters.

Laurie Porter decided at age seven that she would be an artist and a writer when she grew up. She's been a bit of both over the years alongside many other jobs. Recently published in Leaf anthology and on Eclectica, she also has half an MA in creative writing.

Jane Rusbridge has had stories and poems published in various magazines and anthologies, including *The Interpreter's House* and *Mslexia* (2006). She is a Fish Prize winner (2006), a Bridport Prize winner (2003) and she won the Writersinc Writer-of-the-Year award (2005) and was runner up in the Bluechrome Fiction award (2005). She is a creative writing teacher at Chichester University and lives with a farmer and five teenage/young adults by the sea in West Sussex. She has a shed at the bottom of the garden where she writes.

Dimitar Tomov was born in 1957 in the town of Pavlikeni. His books include *Stranger*, a short story collection (1986), *Life Goes On*, a short novel (1990) and *Bulgarian School of Literature* (1997), an essay collection. The story included here, *Road to Brigitte Bardot*, is taken from his latest book *The Eternal Katun* (2004).

Susan Tranter lives in Manchester and works on books and websites. She's Reader in Residence for the British Council's international reading website www.encompassculture.com

Juliet Trewellard comes from Cornwall. She read English at Sussex University and studied theatre at the Central School of Speech and Drama. She worked for several years as an actor and then taught literature and theatre studies. She is a founder member and artistic director of a small South West touring theatre company and she has been writing seriously for the last four years, mainly plays, for both the company and for radio, and short stories and poetry. Her children's novel *Butterfingers* was published in 2007 by David Fickling Books, of Random House. She is currently working on an adult novel.

James K Walker has written freelance and fiction for numerous publications. In 2003 he won the Jo Cowell Award and he is currently researching a book about Brian Clough. When James is not writing he likes to play football with the kids on his street, but refuses to go in goal.

Joby Williams was born in London, and is a graduate from the University of Nottingham. She travels extensively in Latin America and works for a tour company specialising in the region. She is a regular contributor to the books pages of the *Sunday Times* and her short story, 'The Regent's Canal', was long-listed for the Bridport Prize.

Further Short Story Titles

Bonne Route (Route 19)

ISBN: 978-1-901927-34-4

Bonne Route is a book of stories that wander off the beaten track. Short, sharp and full of surprises, these stories reflect on moments which change people's direction in life. Heart-warming and spirited, this collection of modern tales illustrates that it is often the smallest of things that lead us on to a different path – a joke, a letter, a photograph, a drink, a dream.

Ideas Above Our Station (Route 18)

ISBN: 978-1-901927-28-3

Someone is waiting for a train, or it could be a bus or an aeroplane. They are alone. For company, in their coat pocket they are carrying a book of stories. They sit down and take out the book. It falls open on the first page of a new story. What would be the perfect read for them to find there?

Route Compendium (Route 17)

ISBN: 978-1-901927-26-9

A festival of compendium of stories that brings together the first wave of Route's pioneering byteback books. Includes five original collections of contemporary fiction featuring: a showcase of bright young talent; the decorator's tale; stories of love and the trouble it can bring; modern folk tales and a collection of misfits which includes the most audacious car chase short story that you will probably ever read.

Wonderwall (Route 16)

ISBN: 978-1-901927-24-5

This title focuses on the people that matter most in our life; those close at hand – the family member, the friend, the colleague, the passer-by. These stories underline the uniqueness of our own existence, and emphasise that despite our world of instant global communication, it is the real people in our lives who affect us the most.

Naked City (Route 15)

ISBN: 978-1-901927-23-8

At the heart of the modern city we find stories of lovers, stories of people with a desire to connect to someone else, something else. This collection reveals the experience of living through changing times, of people shaking the past and dreaming of better days, people finding their place, adapting to new surroundings, laughing and forgetting, living and loving in the grip of the city. Perhaps there are eight million stories in the naked city. Here are just a few of them.

Next Stop Hope (Route 14)

ISBN: 978-1-901927-19-1

This bumper issue from Route brings together further chronicles of contemporary preoccupations. Presented in three distinct collections: *Criminally Minded*, *Something Has Gone Wrong In The World* and *Next Stop Hope* – this anthology takes you skilfully through the inner workings of the criminal mind, the nuances of human relationships and our personal connections with an increasingly disturbing world, where hope is hard to find.

Recent Route Non-Fiction Titles

Bringing It All Back Home

by Ian Clayton

ISBN: 978-1-901927-35-1

When you hear a certain song, where does it take you? What is the secret that connects music to our lives? Heart-warming, moving and laugh out loud funny, *Bringing It All Back Home* is the truest book you will ever read about music and the things that really matter. Author Ian Clayton listens to music as a kid to escape and as an adult to connect. In *Bringing It All Back Home* he has created a book about love, friendship, family and loss – about life and living it. While searching for a soundtrack to his own life story, he has discovered the heart that beats inside us all.

Made in Bradford

Editor: M Y Alam

ISBN: 978 1 901827-32-0

The aftermath of the Bradford Riots in 2001 and subsequent reports on how the city is constructed, provoked novelist and academic M Y Alam into generating a report of his own. As part of the research process, he spent time interviewing British Pakistani men and gathered their views on issues which are generally prone to misrepresentation elsewhere. *Made In Bradford* compiles a series of transcripts from those conversations and paints a vivid picture of everyday life that reads almost as a counter-narrative to the prevailing direction of current debates. Here, men talk about issues such as forced marriage, drugs and criminality, employment, racism, political representation, the fall out from the London bombings, faith and freedom, along with the notion of home and belonging. The openness within the texts is a refreshing antidote to the recent, more widespread and shameful stigmatisation of a people within our own communities. *Made in Bradford* is an important book of its time.

Comment on Route Series Titles

‘The most interesting and vibrant publishing house around today.’ – **Nottingham Evening Post**

'Route has arrived at a format which could almost be described as a northern *Granta.* For any broad-minded soul that cares to check it out, it remains hard evidence of a valid literary sensibility beyond London.’ – **Artscene**

‘Gleaned from the length and breadth of the UK, these stories do not disappoint. There is a grittiness to these tales, variously dealing in love, and fading or faded dreams and a commendable lack of adornment and sentimentality.’ – **The Glasgow Herald**

‘The sharpest, on the button writing you’ll read all year. Route could soon start taking on a Samizdat level of importance as it quietly ushers in the beginnings of a much needed literary renaissance.’ – **The Big Issue**

‘Punchy, pithy and darkly humorous.’ – **Liverpool Daily Post**

‘A bit like going to a party and meeting one fascinating person after another.’ – **Leeds Guide**

‘Some of the best stories I have ever read.’ – **BBCi**

‘These stories drop you right into what’s going on behind the curtains and in the alleys of your own neighbourhood.’ – **Bradford Telegraph and Argus**

‘The eclectic, the humorous, the heartbreaking, the psychological, the fear and angst are all here in a collection that not only embodies the city but occupies the very soul of the urban landscape.’ – **Inc Writers**

The Route Series

Route publishes a regular series of titles
for which it offers an annual subscription.

Route 1	*Introducing The Graphomaniacs*	February 2000
Route 2	*To The Misomusists*	March 2000
Route 3	*For The Purpose of Healing and Positivity*	April 2000
Route 4	*Believe and Receive*	May 2000
Route 5	*Doubt and Do Without*	June 2000
Route 6	*Start Spreading the News*	July 2000
Route 7	*The B Vocabulary*	October 2000
Route 8	*This Revolution Will Not Be Televised*	December 2000
Route 9	*From The Underground*	March 2001
Route 10	*No Stinking Badges*	May 2001
Route 11	*Welcome Martha Smith*	July 2001
Route 12	*Underwood Monkey Business*	October 2001
Route 13	*From The Wonderland Zoo*	January 2002
Route 14	*Next Stop Hope*	January 2003
Route 15	*Naked City*	October 2004
Route 16	*Wonderwall*	October 2005
Route 17	*Route Compendium*	February 2006
Route 18	*Ideas Above Our Station*	October 2006
Route 19	*Bonne Route*	December 2007

Route Offline (Route 20) is a title in the Route Series.

For details of the current subscription scheme
and complete book list please visit:

www.route-online.com